"Where Are We?"

"My place."

"You said it was a business meeting." Ellen glared at Rudi. She was beautiful when she was angry.

"It is. In town, in the morning." He offered Ellen his hand. "Coming?"

Rudi held his breath as she looked from his face to his hand and back again, waiting for her to decide. Would she take his hand?

When her fingers slid across his palm and her hand closed around his, the touch jolted him. Every molecule in his body wanted her. Not just for sex. He wanted more.

He wanted to see admiration in her eyes. He wanted to hear her laugh. He wanted to wake up with her in the morning after a night of hot, mindless, slow, sultry sex and have her smile at him.

"Well?" Ellen's voice broke into his musing. "Are we going to get off this airplane?"

Rudi grinned. He loved her sass.

Dear Reader,

Welcome to Silhouette Desire, where every month you can count on finding six passionate, powerful and provocative romances.

The fabulous Dixie Browning brings us November's MAN OF THE MONTH, *Rocky and the Senator's Daughter,* in which a heroine on the verge of scandal arouses the protective *and* sensual instincts of a man who knew her as a teenager. Then Leanne Banks launches her exciting Desire miniseries, THE ROYAL DUMONTS, with *Royal Dad*, the timeless story of a prince who falls in love with his son's American tutor.

The Bachelorette, Kate Little's lively contribution to our 20 AMBER COURT miniseries, features a wealthy businessman who buys a date with a "plain Jane" at a charity auction. The intriguing miniseries SECRETS! continues with *Sinclair's Surprise Baby,* Barbara McCauley's tale of a rugged bachelor with amnesia who's stunned to learn he's the father of a love child.

In *Luke's Promise* by Eileen Wilks, we meet the second TALL, DARK & ELIGIBLE brother, a gorgeous rancher who tries to respect his wife-of-convenience's virtue, while *she* looks to *him* for lessons in lovemaking! And, finally, in Gail Dayton's delightful *Hide-and-Sheikh*, a lovely security specialist and a sexy sheikh play a game in which both lose their hearts...and win a future together.

So treat yourself to all six of these not-to-be-missed stories. You deserve the pleasure!

Enjoy,

Joan Marlow Golan

Joan Marlow Golan
Senior Editor, Silhouette Desire

Please address questions and book requests to:
Silhouette Reader Service
U.S.: 3010 Walden Ave., P.O. Box 1325, Buffalo, NY 14269
Canadian: P.O. Box 609, Fort Erie, Ont. L2A 5X3

Hide-And-Sheikh

GAIL DAYTON

Silhouette Desire

Published by Silhouette Books
America's Publisher of Contemporary Romance

SILHOUETTE BOOKS

ISBN 0-373-76404-9

HIDE-AND-SHEIKH

Copyright © 2001 by Gail Shelton

Visit Silhouette at www.eHarlequin.com

Printed in U.S.A.

GAIL DAYTON

has been playing make-believe all her life but didn't start writing the make-believe down until she was about nine years old, because it took her that long to learn how to write coherent sentences. She married her college sweetheart shortly after graduation and moved to a small Central Texas town where they lived happily for twenty years. Now transplanted to an even smaller town in the Texas Panhandle, Gail lives with her Prince Charming, their youngest son and Spot the Dalmatian, where they are still working on the "ever after" part. The "happily" they have down.

After a checkered career with intervals spent as a mommy, the entire editorial staff of more than one small-town newspaper, a junior college history instructor and legal assistant in a rural prosecutor's office, she finally got to quit her day job in favor of writing love stories. When she's not writing or reading other people's love stories, she sings alto in her church choir and teaches basic sewing as an incentive to finish her own sewing projects, which would otherwise languish.

Gail would love to hear from readers. Write her at P.O. Box 176, Clarendon, Texas 79226.

To those wonderful women from Waco,
the best friends a writer could have.
Thanks for all your support. I wouldn't be here
without you. To Myles, for worrying about me when
I don't write, and for twenty-five wonderful years.

One

She'd found her target. He lounged near the make-shift bar, his perfect teeth glinting as he smiled at some dark-haired bimbette. In the warehouse-cum-nightclub in New York's garment district, lights flashed, strobe-quick and bright, or slower, in garish colors that painted the party goers in even more ghastly shades than they'd painted themselves. Except for that man, her night's mission. The Sheikh of Araby.

Or rather, the Sheikh of Qarif, to give him his true name. As she maneuvered her way toward him, Ellen watched the lights turn his handsome face pink, then sickly green, then dappled blue, but his perfection continued unblemished. He knew it, too.

He threw back that chiseled profile in a laugh that had to be calculated to show off his best features: dark sultry eyes, straight white teeth, high, carved cheek-bones. His picture hadn't done him justice.

Oh, it had amply illustrated his movie-star features, but it hadn't said a word about the sexuality that oozed like honey from his every pore. Ellen kept the wry twist from her faint smile at the sight of the little girl bees buzzing around him. She couldn't let him see past the mask she wore to her real purpose. He might be the best-looking, sexiest man she'd seen in the past dozen years, but he was still her target.

And, as mama always said, beauty is skin deep, but ugly goes clear to the bone. Somebody's mama had said it, even if Ellen's never had. She'd known spoiled, rich playboys. One of them she'd known very well.

Davis Lowe had been born with a golden spoon in his mouth and upgraded to platinum at his first op-portunity. He'd swept her off her middle-class feet with his charm and his money and brought her into his world, where she'd met his spoiled playboy friends. Because of Davis, she'd learned these rich men were all the same.

Whether they were from New York or New Delhi, they all expected the world to bow and scrape and cater to their every whim. At least this one offered a nice view.

Finally he reacted to Ellen's laser-beam stare. He looked up and met her gaze. Ellen held it a long mo-ment, allowed a hint of a smile to brush her lips, then she turned away and began to count seconds.

One… She found a place at the sawhorse-and-planking bar, and ordered a gin and tonic. Seven,

eight, nine… Would she have to look at him again?
The pretty ones were often tougher to get to. Ellen
tossed her hair back over her shoulder. Long, straight,
dark blond hair with golden highlights, it was one of
her best weapons.

"Hello."

Bingo. He was hooked. Fourteen seconds. Not her
best time, but not her worst, either. If "the look"
didn't get them, the hair usually did.

Ellen turned and gave her sheikh a once-over. That
high-beam smile of his could prove near lethal at
close range. She raised a cool eyebrow. The effect
was somewhat destroyed by the fact that they had to
lean close and shout full volume to be heard over the
pounding music.

"Hello?" she said. "That's all you can come up
with? What kind of line is that?"

He shrugged. "It is no line. I said hello. If you
want a line, I am sure many other men here would
be happy to provide one."

His English was impeccable, overlaid with a faint
hint of the foreign, and a fainter hint of a…Southern
drawl? He wore a short-sleeved raw silk navy shirt
unbuttoned over a plain white T-shirt. A T-shirt that
must have been bought a size too small, given the
way it strained over the man's lean but well-muscled
torso. Khaki slacks finished the ensemble. Not what
one would expect from the scion of a royal family,
but it looked good on him. Darn good. Did she have
the right man? Ellen studied his face again, compar-
ing it to the memorized photo in her head. This *was*
her target. No mistake.

She lifted a shoulder in a casual shrug. Cool and calculated would serve her better with this one. He would be used to women falling over themselves to please him.

"I don't need a line." She accepted the drink from the bartender and took a sip, schooling her expression against the taste. Fruity concoctions with paper umbrellas, the kind she preferred, didn't blend with the sophisticated image she wanted to project tonight.

He grinned and pushed his hand back through his thick sable hair. "That is just as well," he said, "because I do not have any idea what to say next. Whatever I say will sound like a pick-up line."

Ellen found herself charmed by his apparent openness and told herself it was an act. It had to be. Nobody with "prince" in front of his name could be this transparent.

"Have you any suggestions?" He propped an elbow on the bar and leaned. The wattage in his smile seemed to go up.

"My name is Ellen." She put her hand out to shake. She had to keep him on a string until she knew she could reel him in.

"Names. Good." He took her hand and squeezed gently. "Call me Rudy."

Rudy? Ellen ran through the list of names they'd given her, half a dozen or more, all belonging to the target. Of the few she could actually remember, Rashid was one, and it didn't sound anything like Rudy. Neither did any of the others.

"Rudi, with an *i*," he said. "I prefer the way it looks written that way."

She shook the hand still holding hers. "How do you do, Rudi-with-an-*i*. It's nice to meet you."

Whatever he wanted to call himself made no difference to her. But it did surprise her a bit. Why not use his real name? Unless he was more security conscious than he appeared. Ellen stopped herself from searching the room for bodyguards. She knew where his bodyguards were. She'd sent them there herself.

"So." He glanced down at their still-clasped hands, and the brilliance of his smile suddenly took on a heat that Ellen felt clear down to her toes, which curled in their strappy sandals. "Now that we have the formalities over, why don't we…"

His words trailed off as he bent over her hand and pressed a kiss to its back, a kiss that sizzled across her skin straight to the libido she'd thought long ago starved to death.

Why don't we *what?* Curiosity resurrected her dormant desire. Nothing else had for years.

"Dance," Rudi said.

"Dance?" That's all he wanted to do?

Feeling numb and yet feeling every nerve ending spark and sizzle, Ellen let him lead her by the hand— the same hand he'd kissed—onto the dance floor. Rudi tugged, spinning her skillfully into his arms. Never mind that the band clashed and wailed and thumped out raging heavy metal rock that made the flashing lights shudder with vibration. Rudi held her close and danced what Ellen could only describe as some kind of cross between a tango, a foxtrot and sex with clothes on.

Or maybe the sex part was just in her head.

This dance, seen objectively, wasn't much different from the hundreds of others Ellen had danced. Rudi's hands rested lightly at her waist, her hands on his shoulders. They moved back and forth to the music in the limited space allowed on the crowded dance floor. But with every brush of Rudi's hips against hers, the heat turned a notch higher.

Ellen's hands curved over Rudi's shoulders, shaping themselves to his lean musculature. He was sleek and strong, beautiful like one of those horses they raised in his part of the world.

He laughed, a very male sound, his eyes flashing pleasure at her, and Ellen realized her hands had slipped. Now they rested on the broad slope of his chest. With another laugh, Rudi whipped off the unbuttoned shirt he wore to let the T-shirt beneath show off his physique. Ellen didn't have to fake her approval. She liked the way he looked. Entirely too much.

He snapped out one end of the shirt, reached out and caught the other end so that it passed behind Ellen. Then he used it to draw her in closer, until they touched hip to hip. Holding her only with the shirt pulled snug around her waist, Rudi swayed, his eyes twinkling.

"Join me," he shouted over the crashing music. "Do you not know how to rumba?"

She pushed at him, her fingers curling into his chest. "This doesn't sound like a rumba to me."

Rudi deepened the swing of his hips, his thighs getting friendly with their sensual nudging against hers. "The beat is in your blood. Feel it inside you."

Was it getting hotter in here? Or was he just making her crazy?

He leaned in, until his lips brushed her ear. ''Feel it, and let it out.''

Rudi did something with his hands, and the shirt around her jumped several inches higher, drawing her slowly in, bringing her breasts toward that white-clad chest.

Confusion struck her. This was a new dilemma. She needed to tempt him, keep him close until the final moment. But she'd never before been tempted herself. She wanted to touch him, to let her breasts settle against that solid chest, and that would be entirely unethical. She wasn't supposed to like her targets.

The music paused to allow the gasping musicians time to catch their collective breath. In the startling, deafening silence, Ellen broke away, tugging the navy shirt from his hands. She stared at him, panting almost as hard as the band. Why? She hadn't done anything strenuous.

Rudi's smile faltered a second, then returned. ''Let me buy you a drink.'' The white of his T-shirt contrasted with his deep tan. He was gorgeous *and* nice. A deadly combination.

Ellen had to get this done and get out quickly, before she got in over her head. It was for his own good. And for hers. They'd both be better off if she just got it over with now.

''I have a better idea.'' Still holding his shirt, Ellen caught Rudi's hand and led him from the dance floor.

''Where are we going?''

"You'll see." She threw him one of her patented mysterious smiles, her hair swinging around her shoulders.

Rudi followed her out of the warehouse, bemused by his luck. Ellen was the most beautiful woman he'd seen in his entire life, and he'd seen a lot of beautiful women. But they never came on to him like this. Not to Rudi.

Only Rashid ibn Saqr ibn Faruq al Mukhtar Qarif could get women at the snap of his fingers. And then it was the money and the power that attracted them, not the man.

Money and power were as much of an illusion as Rashid. Or maybe Rudi was the illusion. Sometimes he wasn't sure which of his personas was the real one. But he did know that the money and the power belonged to his father, not to him.

Down the street outside the warehouse, Ellen hailed a taxi. The streetlight gleamed along her slender, mile-high legs as she got in. Rudi stared, half-hypnotized, until Ellen leaned out the open car door.

"Are you coming?" she asked, a smile curving her luscious pink lips. A smile that promised nothing and everything at the same time, that dared him to find out what secrets hid behind it.

He shouldn't. He had doubtless terrified and infuriated his family enough, vanishing as he had. The bombs back in Qarif were real. The terrorists were real. But the terrorists were still in Qarif, trying to transform the country into a miniature Afghanistan. This woman could not possibly be a terrorist. Just look at her.

Rudi followed his own suggestion as she waited without a hint of impatience for him to make up his mind. She was a blond goddess, a Valkyrie escaped from Wagner's opera. Her straight dark gold hair spilled over her shoulders like yesterday's sunlight, streaked with the brighter shine of tomorrow's dawn. Long thick lashes shaded eyes whose color he couldn't decipher in the uncertain light. A high forehead, straight narrow nose, prominent cheekbones and full mouth completed her classically beautiful face.

But it was not the beauty of her face or her sleek athlete's body beneath the simple black dress that drew him. Perhaps it was the hint of mischief in her eyes, or the mystery in her smile, the feeling that she played some secret game and he did not know the rules. She challenged him, dared him to play. Rudi had never been able to pass up a dare.

He stepped off the curb and got in the cab. Satisfaction flickered across Ellen's face a brief second before she hid it behind that smile. Rudi did not object. She had won only one hand. He intended to win the game.

"So, Rudi." Ellen leaned back in the corner of the cab opposite him. "What do you do?"

"I dig holes." At least, he wanted to. His family did their level best to keep him in a nice, clean office where he couldn't play in the dirt.

Ellen's eyebrow arched. "Really."

Would she back off now, thinking him no more than a ditchdigger?

"Holes, as in the Lincoln Tunnel?" she asked. "Or holes as in—" She waved at a construction site vanishing behind them, where bulldozers would have clawed deep into the earth to set the foundation before the steel frame started up.

"Holes as in wells. For water, oil—whatever is hiding down there."

Ellen's expression changed, as if she were impressed in spite of herself. At least, Rudi hoped that was what it meant.

"You dig oil wells?" She stretched a long, elegant arm along the back of the seat.

Rudi started to agree, then changed his mind. Tell her the truth, see how that impressed her. If it did. "Actually, I prefer drilling for water. A person cannot drink oil."

"You can't run a car on water."

"Not now." Rudi grinned. "Give the scientists some time. If they ever finish their fusion reactor research, we could be pulling up to the garden hose to fill our cars with fuel."

She watched him with that enigmatic smile on her face, saying nothing. Rudi did not know if that meant she wanted to know more or was bored to tears. But he did not handle silence well.

"Of course, you can make more money drilling oil wells, but…" Rudi shrugged. "The people who need water generally need it more."

Ellen's smile changed, became warmer and yet sad at the same time. This smile still hid secrets, but it seemed more genuine. "You're a nice man, Rudi," she said. "I like you."

Stunned, Rudi didn't realize the cab had stopped until Ellen got out. Scrambling to follow her beckoning gesture, he found himself on the sidewalk in front of an upscale hotel. Ellen linked her arm through his and strolled past the doorman into the gilt-and-marble lobby.

She led him past the desk, past the plush brocade chairs, past the opening to the dimly lit bar, to the elevators between the potted palms where she pushed the up button. Rudi's second thoughts kicked in.

Not that he objected to the idea of going up to Ellen's room and "getting to know her better." But he did not know her. She probably was no terrorist. Then again, she might be. Or she might be a thief, with a partner upstairs waiting to cosh him over the head and steal everything he had in his pockets, which by now was not much, since he had been away from the family coffers for more than a week.

Or she might be the best thing he had ever happened across in his life.

He was used to women throwing themselves at him, wanting to be seen with him for his name, or his money, or because they liked the way he looked. Their motivations had always been transparent to him, and he'd usually been willing to give them what they wanted—a little pleasure for the moment, a little thrill, a little pampering. They were easy. So easy that lately he hadn't bothered.

But this woman was different. She intrigued him. She challenged him by holding her secrets so close. She was all mystery and potential and wide-open possibility.

In which case, he did not want to ruin it by rushing into sex with her. He wanted to know more, know everything about her, how she thought, what made her laugh and cry. That took time. If he went upstairs with her now, Rudi very much feared he wouldn't get that time.

"Ellen, why do we not go into the bar? Have a drink. Talk." He tipped his head toward the dark, cavelike entrance.

Something that might have been surprise flashed in her eyes before it vanished behind that sexy, enigmatic smile. Rudi began to hate that smile.

"Why?" She slid her hand up his arm to his shoulder and trailed her fingers down his chest.

"I wish to talk to you." He caught the hand resting on his chest and kissed her fingertips. Then he touched the corner of her mouth.

Her smile slipped, just a little.

"I want to find the woman behind that smile," he said. "If we go upstairs, I do not think that we will do very much talking."

"Probably not," Ellen conceded with a tip of her head. "But what if there's nothing to find?"

"I cannot believe that. Not with the devil peeking from deep within your eyes."

An expression that was almost alarm flickered in those hazel-green eyes. Then her smile went hot and sultry, and Rudi's entire body stood at attention.

"Talking isn't the way to meet that devil." Ellen took both his hands in hers and backed onto the elevator, drawing him with her. "We can talk later."

"Promise?"

The elevator door slid shut. Ellen brushed against Rudi as she reached past him to press a floor button, and he shuddered at the light touch. His hand settled at her waist.

"I promise," she said.

Rudi had to think a minute to recall what she was promising.

"If you still want to talk, we can talk all you want. Later."

The floor lurched slightly as the elevator stopped and the door rumbled open. Holding his hand, Ellen led him into the hallway. About halfway down, she paused in front of a room.

She looked up at him, the sweet sadness back in her smile. Her hand settled soft on his chest again, and she stretched the mere inch necessary to touch her lips to his cheek in a warm, tender kiss that melted all Rudi's internal organs together.

She glanced away to slide the keycard in the lock. It flashed green and she turned the handle, then looked back up at him.

"I'm sorry," she murmured, "but it's for your own good."

Alarm flashed through him. Was she a terrorist after all?

Then the door was open and Omar, his valet-cum-bodyguard, was hauling him into the room. Frank, the rent-a-bodyguard from the service his family used in New York, stood behind Omar, with a third burly guard beyond.

"Thanks, Miss Sheffield," Frank was saying. "I knew if anybody could find him, you could."

Ellen's smile was gone, replaced by a businesslike

scowl. "I wouldn't have had to, if you bozos hadn't lost him in the first place."

"You are a bodyguard?" Rudi goggled at her.

"I'm a security consultant. Frank and George are bodyguards." She indicated the two locals. "See if you can keep up with him now."

And she was gone, the door slamming shut behind her.

The woman of his dreams had come on to him just to track him down for his family and return him to the dubious safety of his bodyguards.

Rudi started to laugh. He had to—she had outwitted him so cleverly. She had won this round.

But the game was not over yet.

And she had promised him they could talk later, if he wished. Rudi definitely wished to talk much more with Miss Ellen Sheffield.

Two

Ellen Sheffield was the best at what she did.

At least, she used to be, before she met that too-handsome-for-her-own-good son of a sheikh. His movie-star face kept popping into her head, complete with that obnoxious grin. The one that made him look even more handsome. No matter how hard she tried to dismiss him as a lightweight, tell herself the grin was goofy and the man uninteresting, his voice would whisper in her mind's ear, *A person cannot drink oil.* And she'd wonder if he still wanted to talk.

Because, however many times she told herself she didn't want to see him, she couldn't forget that he had actually wanted to delay going upstairs at the hotel. He'd invited her into the bar. He'd seen past the mask to the person behind her polished facade, the first man to bother looking in years. Maybe ever.

When she was little, she'd been merely "the Sheffield boys' sister." Then she'd grown breasts, and her brothers' friends had done nothing but stare at them. Until her brothers beat them up.

None of the boys in high school had dared ask her out, and with a policeman for a brother, none of the men in the academy had, either. So she'd had no preparation for Davis's practiced seduction when she'd met him at a book signing just after she'd finished her course.

Ellen sighed. Davis had been such an overwhelming experience that she'd agreed to marry him before she realized what kind of man he was. Before she realized what kind of woman he wanted. He wanted a decorative, expensive toy to show off to his friends, not a person. Ellen's opinions, desires, thoughts and wishes had all been dismissed as unimportant. Her career was immaterial. Davis expected her to drop everything and dance to his tune.

When she'd broken the engagement, his "friends" had moved in, all of them wanting the same thing: a beautiful woman to show off. She'd learned then how to use her appearance as a tool, a weapon against them. That skill had benefited her career, both in the police department and since. Vic Campanello, her partner on the job and her current boss, called her his secret weapon. Which was why she'd been tapped to find Prince Rudi the Gorgeous.

She didn't want to think about him, didn't want him popping into her head. He might have noticed the devil in her eyes, but he couldn't care anymore.

Not now, not after she'd put him back into his gilded cage.

Ellen got out of the cab and slammed the door. Then she overtipped the driver because she felt guilty for taking out her guilt on his cab. She had not betrayed Rudi, or Rashid, or whatever the man wanted to call himself. She had probably saved his life. He had no business wandering around New York on his own, not with terrorists stalking Qarif's ruling family, of which Rudi was most definitely a member.

The terrorists had been a problem in Qarif for most of Rudi's life, but lately things had changed, according to Campanello. The old leader had been captured, and the new, more militant leader had vowed vengeance for the captivity, even though he was probably the one who'd tipped the authorities off.

Rudi might be used to the terrorist threat, but that didn't mean there was no danger. Ellen's job was to protect him from that danger, and she had absolutely no reason to feel guilty for doing her job.

Summer flowers bloomed in beds lining the paths, but they might as well have been weeds for all the attention Ellen paid them as she headed into Central Park. She checked her watch and picked up her pace. If she didn't hurry, she'd be late for her meeting.

Swainson Security had been hired to provide security for a music video to be shot in Central Park sometime in the next month, and she was supposed to meet with the producer, the director, the group's manager and whoever else thought they needed a finger in the pie, to check out locations. She much preferred this kind of work to tracking down spoiled dilettantes. Though she had to admit that finding Rudi had been a challenge. She did enjoy a good challenge.

Campanello had told her this morning he had a new assignment for her, one that would begin immediately after this meeting. Maybe it would offer something tough enough to keep her mind off Qarif's prince. The fact that the boss wouldn't tell her what the new job was, however, made her suspect that it might have something to do with said prince.

Ellen ground her teeth, then curled her lips up in what she hoped resembled a smile more than a snarl as the band's manager turned to greet her. Time to go to work.

Rudi stared at the piece of paper in front of him on the polished table without actually seeing it or anything it said. It was Wednesday. Hump Day, as they had called it when he was in college in Texas, and probably everywhere else in the United States. If he could make it past Wednesday, it was a downhill slide to the weekend. Only, the weekend would be no better, trapped as he was by his bodyguards and big brother Ibrahim.

Rudi felt Ibrahim's glower and ignored it. He pulled his hand inside the sleeve of his djellaba and discreetly scratched his thigh. Ibrahim had insisted on traditional dress for the negotiations today, to remind the other parties just who they dealt with. Rudi stuck his hand back out and took yet another sip of water. Maybe he could escape to the rest room for a few minutes, if he drank enough water.

He had no idea why he had to be at this forsaken

meeting anyway. It was not as if he could contribute anything but another body. Ibrahim's wife or one of his children now in New York could contribute as much. Rudi would happily trade places with Kalila and escort the children to museums and even opera, while she sat in on her husband's meetings. They were about finance and numbers, dollars and marks and yen and things he knew nothing about. Did not want to know about.

Give him a piece of ground, a "Christmas tree" rig and a couple of roughnecks to handle the steel, and he could bring in the well. He could even tell you if the piece of ground might produce anything, whether water, oil or gas. But high finance could kill him. If Rudi got any more bored, his heart just might forget to beat, fall asleep just like the rest of him. Although if he actually dozed off, Ibrahim would be the one to kill him.

He had sworn off thinking about her. This resolution had lasted about as long as every other resolution he had ever made. Maybe an entire hour. He needed something to do that would keep him awake, so he began to plot his revenge on Ellen Sheffield. Most of the plots involved isolated tents in the desert, paved with thick, soft carpets and plenty of pillows, and thin, gauzy, semitransparent clothing. Better yet, no clothing at all.

Not that the plots would ever come to fruition. It had been ten days since Ellen had turned him back over to the loving, suffocating arms of his family like a runaway schoolboy, and he still had no hint how to find her. Her company "did not give out personal information,'' as he had been told several times over by the annoying, perky-voiced receptionist. His dream girl might have been just that—a dream—for all he was able to learn about her. He had held her in his arms, only to have her vanish like a mirage in the sands.

''What is your opinion, Prince Rashid?''

One of the suits around the table asked him a question, and Rudi had no idea what he was supposed to have an opinion about. Even if he had heard the discussion, he would not have understood it. He moved his leg out of reach of Ibrahim's potential kick under the table.

''I am in complete agreement with my brother,'' he said, which was true. Ibrahim knew about this kind of thing. Rudi wished he would take care of it and stop making him sit through this agony.

Finally, after another eternity of congratulations and chitchat and backslapping, the deal apparently made, the meeting ended. Rudi headed for the elevators, only to be halted by his brother calling him back.

''Rashid, are you not joining us for lunch?'' Ibrahim looked surprised, maybe even wounded by Rudi's apparent defection. ''To celebrate the success of our negotiations. Come.''

Allah forfend. Rudi stifled his shudder. He could not take another hour of high finance, not another minute. He had been to lunch with these men before. He knew what they talked about.

''Forgive me, brother. It has been a long morning, and I feel a bit under the weather.''

"Are you ill?" Genuine concern colored Ibrahim's voice.

Rudi was grateful once more that he was merely the seventh son of his father, and not the ninth and youngest. If young Hasim stubbed a toe, the flags in Qarif went to half-mast. Ibrahim would have panicked.

"Merely tired." Rudi said. "I will catch a cab back to the hotel."

"You will take the car. And Omar."

"Very well. I will take the car." Rudi did not mention that Omar was back at the hotel with a severe case of traveler's trouble, and had only consented to stay in bed because of Ibrahim's own bodyguards. This could be his chance to make a break for it.

Maybe they would send Ellen after him again.

Rudi was whistling by the time he reached the garage.

He slouched in the back seat of the bulletproof, bombproof, escapeproof car, and plotted his escape. Without Omar, or any of the rent-a-bodies, it ought to be relatively easy. He had received a phone call from Buckingham, saying that everything was ready and just waiting for him. He could get the driver to drop him at the hotel, catch a cab to the heliport and take a helicopter to the airport. He could be gone without anyone knowing it. Perhaps they would send Ellen after him again. Perhaps he would allow her to find him.

But not in Buckingham. No one knew about Buckingham, and that was the way he wanted it.

Then he sat up straight, his attention captured by a woman in the park as the car inched along in the near-noon traffic. It was Ellen. It had to be. No other woman could possibly possess that precise combination of sun-kissed hair and million-dollar legs.

She was talking with an odd collection of mostly men. Or rather Ellen stood near them while they talked. She did not seem to be paying much attention, looking at her surroundings, until one of the men put his arm around her. Ellen moved away from his arm, but listened to what he had to say, nodding now and again.

The car moved a few feet ahead, leaving Ellen and the rest of the group walking slowly the other way. Rudi turned to watch, swearing when his view was blocked by a horse and rider.

In that instant, a plan sprang full-grown into his head. He had always wanted to sweep a woman off her feet and carry her away on horseback, like his great-grandfathers had surely once done. He was even dressed for it, in his desert robes.

"Stop." Rudi didn't wait for the driver to comply. The car was barely moving as he opened the door. "I will be back in five minutes, perhaps ten."

He caught up with the horseback rider in a few quick steps, wondering if he ought to rethink his plan. This horse seemed to have little in common with the fiery animals in his father's stables. He caught the beast's rein, startling a little shriek from its rider, a slightly plump, barely pubescent girl with braces and red frizz under a white helmet.

"Hello, might I borrow your horse?" Rudi bor-

rowed Ibrahim's Oxford accent. It seemed to play better dressed as he was. "I wish to surprise my fian-
cée." The lie rolled easily from his lips. "By
sweeping her away in the manner of my ancestors."

The girl gulped and giggled. Rudi captured her
hand. "Surely someone of your sensibility would be
willing to assist in my romantic endeavors." His ploy
seemed to be working on the horse's rider.

"I've only got an hour to ride," she said.

"I only need the barest minute." Rudi glanced
over his shoulder. Ellen and her party were retreating
deeper into the park. In a moment they would be out
of sight. "Please. My heart will be devastated if you
do not allow me the use of your steed for a paltry
space of time." Maybe those English literature
classes he had suffered through had done better work
than he had thought.

"My heart is in your hands." Rudi pressed a kiss
to the child's hand, and she giggled again, looking
past him at a cluster of other riders who had pulled
up to stare gape-mouthed at the scene he was making.

She sighed. "Okay. But just a minute." She slid
awkwardly from the horse's back.

"Allah bless you for your generosity." Rudi kissed
her cheek, knowing it would impress the girl's audi-
ence, then swung into the saddle.

The horse recognized a knowledgeable hand on the
reins and took exception. It preferred being in charge.
But after a brief, stern scolding, Rudi reminded the
animal of its manners, and it did as he demanded.

Payback would be sweet indeed.

* * *

Ellen walked back toward the fountain with all the video people, only half listening to their chatter of angles and dollies and dance steps as she mentally placed barricades and personnel across park paths and lawns. So hard did she concentrate on blocking out all the extraneous noise that she didn't hear the hoofbeats until they were almost on top of her.

The sudden thunder brought her whirling around to see a horse bearing down on her, on its back a man in the billowing white robes of a desert nomad.

"Crazy son of a—" The producer had no time to finish his oath before diving aside.

Too surprised to move, Ellen watched the man lean toward her, saw his arm stretch out. Before she could react, he'd snatched her from her feet and hauled her up onto the horse in front of him. Her mind was so muddled, she could only think what an impressive feat he'd just accomplished.

Voices rose about them, shouting. "Call 9-1-1!"

"He's crazy! Somebody stop him."

"He's kidnapping her!"

The horse's stride shortened abruptly, then it whirled and galloped back the way it had come. Ellen clung to the man to keep from flying off during the sharp turn, noticing despite herself the lean, almost familiar strength of his body. Who was this nutcase? She was afraid she already knew.

She batted the windblown robes out of her way and looked up into the face that had been haunting her dreams. Rudi.

If the cops arrested him, it could create an international incident. It could get her fired.

"It's okay," she shouted past his shoulder at the video crew. "I know him. He's a friend."

Her words apparently reached them, because the frantic shouting and rushing slowed. The horse didn't.

Its rocking gait bumped her against Rudi in a matching rhythm, a rhythm that came too easily to mind in connection with this man. No wonder the body beneath the robes had felt so familiar. Hard as she tried, she hadn't been able to forget the feel of him under her hands. The muscular thighs that had teased her in that blood-boiling dance now flexed and shifted beneath her, guiding a thousand-plus pounds of horseflesh, pushing their way back into her memory.

"Am I truly?" He grinned at her, his teeth flashing white in the afternoon sun as the horse thundered on across the park.

"Are you truly what?" Ellen pried her brain away from the legs beneath her backside and ordered it to get busy with thinking.

"Your friend. You said I was a friend."

"I—" *Think.* She wanted to bang her head against something to see if she could knock a little sense loose, but the nearest something was Rudi's chest, and she knew beyond any doubt that would only make things worse. "I didn't want you arrested."

"Ah." His Day-Glo smile dimmed a fraction.

The horse came to a skittering halt at a signal from Rudi that Ellen missed. He dismounted and tossed the reins to a waiting child before lifting Ellen from the horse's back. But instead of setting her on her feet, he carried her in his arms to a car at the curb. The driver opened the door, and Rudi put her inside, much the same way Ellen had once inserted prisoners into her patrol car. Before following her inside, Rudi called to the girl with the horse.

"Blessings upon you, child." He tossed her a coin that glinted gold as it spun over and over in a high arc. Ellen saw the girl miss the catch and bend to pick it up before Rudi got into the car and signaled to the driver.

"What was that you threw?" Ellen asked.

"A ten-fiat piece."

"It looked like gold."

"It is." Rudi stretched his arms along the seat and the door, looking completely at ease in his exotic garb. He seemed a different person somehow. Strange, foreign, exciting.

"Gold." She had to get a grip on this situation. She had to get a grip on herself.

He made an affirming hum. "I wanted to reward her for the loan of the horse."

"With a ten-fiat gold piece."

He mmm-ed again in agreement.

"How much is that in real money?"

Rudi laughed. "Some people would say that the fiat is real money, since it is actually gold and not your paper greenbacks."

"How much?" Ellen didn't know why she persisted, only that she wanted to know. Maybe her brain was trying to get warmed up.

"Depending on a number of factors, between thirty and fifty dollars, American."

Resentment swelled inside her. Did he think he

could impress her by throwing his money around like that? Or did he think to buy her, the way he'd bought the use of the horse?

"What do you want?" Ellen didn't care if her attitude sounded in her voice.

"A bit of your time." Rudi's voice seemed calculated to soothe, and so rubbed her resentment raw. "You did promise me we could talk, remember?"

She did, and resented even more being put in the wrong. "If you wanted to talk to me, all you had to do was call the office and say so."

"I did. You have not been taking my calls."

He was right again. Another mark against him.

"So talk." She slouched in the seat, tugging at the hem of her dress. It drew his eyes to her legs where they emerged from the short skirt, and his gaze heated the atmosphere.

"I want more than a few stolen minutes in the back of a car," Rudi said.

I just bet you do. Ellen shot him a sideways glance and met his gaze looking back. He knew how guilty she felt, the rat, and was playing it for all he was worth. She wanted to kiss that smirk—no. No, she wanted to wipe that smirk off his face. Wipe. She didn't dare think of Rudi and kissing in the same thought.

"I have received a call concerning some business I must take care of out of the city this afternoon. I want you to come with me." Rudi watched her like a cat near an active mouse hole.

Ellen was already shaking her head. "No, I'm sorry. It's impossible."

"Why?" Rudi slid a finger across the curve of her bare shoulder.

She shoved his hand away as she repressed her shuddering reaction. "I have responsibilities. A job. And you have other bodyguards." Her eyes narrowed. "Speaking of which, where are they?"

"Omar is sick, the others are with Ibrahim. The driver is driving."

"That's no good. You should have at least one other guard with you at all times."

Rudi's smile glistened in the car's dim light. "You are with me."

"I'm not your bodyguard."

"Why not? Come with me. I have cleared it with your company. I have cleared it with my family. All is prepared." He paused and gave her a little-boy-pleading-for-a-treat look. "That is, if you agree."

"What if I don't?" Ellen fought against the temptation. If she wanted something this much, it had to be bad for her. But what if this was the new job Campanello wanted her on?

"I will have the driver drop you wherever you want to go." The teasing grin was back. "Preferably after lunch. Grant me at least that much."

She eyed him, all her suspicion sensors on alert. "What about you? If I don't go, who will you take on your trip?"

"Myself."

Scowling, Ellen decided not to argue with him. He was just contrary enough to do what he threatened. If she didn't go, he'd go alone, and that was absolutely out of the question. "I want to call my office, make sure this is okay with my boss."

Rudi's expression didn't change, didn't even flicker as he gave a nonchalant shrug. Either he really had cleared it with everyone, or he was a consummate actor. "Of course. Whatever you think you need to do." He handed her a cell phone from somewhere inside those voluminous robes.

"Thanks. I have my own." Ellen pulled her phone from the bag she'd somehow hung on to when Rudi snatched her up on the horse. She had to think a minute to remember the office number. How could this man interfere so with her thought process?

"Swainson Security." The phone was answered on the first ring.

"Hey, Marco. Is Campanello in?"

"Oh, hey, Ms. Sheffield. No, he's out meeting with those guys about that string concert in October."

"String?" Ellen racked her brain trying to recall any violinists the company had contracted with. "Do you mean Sting?"

"Maybe that's what he said. I just know it was some old guy. But he did tell me to tell you those sheikhs wanted you to head up the detail for—uh—" The rustle of paper shuffling came through the phone. "For one of them. I can't find the paper with the guy's name on it. It was here just a minute ago." Marco sounded stressed.

Ellen glanced at Rudi. She hated being pushed into things. But he was the client, and clients had the right to do a limited amount of pushing. "Tell Campanello I know about it, and I'm on the job."

It had to be Rudi they wanted her with. Campanello had been bugging her about it ever since she'd found the man. Ellen didn't do guard details anymore if she could help it, but it didn't look as if she could help this one. Rudi had boxed her in.

"Got it, Ms. Sheffield."

"I'm going to try to reach the boss on his cell phone, but if I can't, tell him I'll check in again as soon as I can. Everything's under control. I've got Rudi with me."

"I'll be sure to tell him. Rudi."

"Thanks." Ellen flipped the phone shut and tucked it away.

"Marco—another hulking brute like Frank or George?" Rudi's eyes twinkled at her. "Or someone more interesting?"

"Definitely more interesting." Ellen chuckled. "He's sixteen. A friend of one of Campanello's kids. It's his first summer job. He might be hulking someday, after he gains a hundred pounds. He's a good kid. And he only answers the phones during lunch."

"Ah." Rudi leaned forward and gave the driver an address. Ellen didn't hear it clearly. "Speaking of lunch, do you mind if we eat on the way? It will save some time."

"Sure, why not? What's a few crumbs on the upholstery?"

The driver let them off at an uptown building Ellen wasn't familiar with. She got on the elevator with Rudi, forcing herself to go into bodyguard mode. She hadn't done this kind of work in a while, but it had been even longer since she'd been in date mode. Besides, this wasn't a date.

As they traveled upward, Rudi excused himself and stepped away to make a few calls. He was still talking when the elevator stopped at the top floor, and Ellen stepped out first, like a good bodyguard, into the small, glass-walled enclosure.

Correction. This wasn't the top floor. They were on the roof, in the lobby area of a heliport. Ellen had been in most of New York's heliports, but not this one. Rudi shut off his phone and strode to the desk, Ellen at his elbow.

"Your helicopter is waiting, Mr. Ibn Saqr," the clerk said, gesturing out the window.

There it was, a shiny white helicopter just settling to the pad as if conjured up by a genie's magic.

"Shall we?" Rudi bowed slightly, offering his arm.

Ellen ignored it, striding to the door. "Don't waste your gallantry on me," she said, pushing the door open.

The roar of helicopter blades vibrated through the little lobby until Rudi pulled the door shut again. Ellen let him. Let him have his say without shouting.

"Gallantry is never wasted on a beautiful woman," he said with a little bow.

Ellen rolled her eyes and shoved at the door again. She was sick of being beautiful, sick of people who could see nothing else. Agreeing to come on this trip was a mistake. She should have known Rudi would be just like all the other men she'd ever met. She stalked out the door and climbed into the helicopter. Just do the job. Ignore the charm. It wasn't for her, but for the mask she wore.

Three

Wind whipped Rudi's djellaba into a tangle as he hurried behind Ellen to the helicopter. He almost shivered in the sudden chill emanating from her. What had he said, what could he possibly have done to plunge her into this icy mood?

He had called her beautiful. What woman could object to that? She was beautiful. Stunningly so. She was also clever, responsible and determined. But beyond that, Rudi thought he had seen a vulnerability in her. A softness beneath the polished surface waiting for someone—the right man—to find it. He wanted to be that man.

The helicopter landed at the airport outside the city where he kept his private plane. Ellen balked as he led her across the tarmac to where the plane waited, engines thrumming.

"Just exactly how far is this place we're going?" she demanded.

"Not far. Wink of an eye and we will be there." He urged her onward, and reluctantly she came.

"Then why do we need to take a plane?"

"So we can get there in the wink of an eye. Without the plane it would be four winks and a snore, at least." Rudi tried teasing to pull her out of that icebox.

She humphed and climbed on board. The plane's opulent appointments irritated Rudi less than usual, because he hoped they might soothe Ellen's mood. Technically the plane belonged to the family, for ferrying various members here and there, but practically it belonged to Rudi. He was, for the most part, the only one who used it. Everyone else preferred to use the larger, even more luxurious model. Rudi liked this one, the smallest jet the company made, because he could fly it himself if he wanted.

The lunch basket was in place on the table, he noted as he paused to pull off his robes. He draped them over one of the seats and headed forward, wearing only the dark slacks and white dress shirt that were his usual attire beneath the djellaba.

"Samuel." Rudi clapped his hand on the pilot's shoulder. "Is everything ready?"

"All set. You're flying yourself?"

"I am." Rudi took the clipboard from the other man. "Take the day off. Take the week off, if you prefer."

Samuel laughed. "Maybe I'd better. You're skipping out again, aren't you?"

Rudi kept his expression bland. "I have a body-guard with me."

Disbelieving, the pilot bent and looked into the passenger cabin. He straightened with a low whistle. "Some bodyguard. I wouldn't mind guarding that body any day."

"That body is guarding me, and from what I hear, she is very, very good at it."

"You'll have to tell me all about it when you get back."

Rudi gave the other man a look calculated to intimidate. It did not work as intended—nothing much intimidated Samuel—but at least he fell silent. "Did you get the flight plan filed for me?"

"Barely. You didn't give much notice." Samuel paused. "Santa Fe again?"

"That is what the flight plan says." Rudi bent over the instruments, beginning his preflight checklist.

"So how come every time you file a flight plan to Santa Fe, you never get there?"

Though his heart pounded with nerves, just as it had when Ellen called her office, Rudi refused to let it show. He trusted Sam with his life, but not with his privacy. No one knew where he was going, and it would stay that way. He had somehow made it past Ellen's phone call without catastrophe striking. He would survive this, too. "I get there. Sometimes."

"Not often."

"Often enough." Rudi straightened and turned to face Samuel. "It is no business of yours, is it?"

"It is if I get fired for not doing my job. You know

I'm supposed to stay with the plane, even if you're flying. I belong in the right-hand seat.''

"We have done this for years. No one has ever caught on, and no one will now. If they do, if they fire you, I will hire you.''

"You can't afford me.'' Samuel met Rudi's gaze for a long challenging moment before he looked away. "But it's your business. Just don't get me caught up in it.''

"I am doing nothing illegal, nor is it immoral. I simply need room to breathe every now and again.''

"Okay, okay. With these terrorists running around back in Qarif, you can't blame a guy for worrying.''

Rudi winked. "That is why I am taking a body-guard with me this time.''

Samuel winked back. "Sure it is. Right.'' He drew the word out long with skepticism. He left the cockpit then, and Rudi followed.

"I will see you in a few days,'' Rudi said quietly, as Samuel stepped off the plane.

"There's a thunderstorm brewing beyond Harris-burg,'' Samuel said. "Better keep an eye on it.''

"Thank you. I will.'' Rudi hauled up the door and dogged it shut, then turned to see Ellen watching him.

"Isn't he the pilot?''

"I am.'' Rudi plucked an apple from the basket and bit into it. "Fully qualified with all the required certificates. I learned to fly during my military train-ing several years ago. I flew this plane here from Qarif.''

Ellen eyed him as if she were having second thoughts about agreeing to the trip.

"Do you want me to call you a cab?" he asked. "I am going, whether you come or not. So do I go with a bodyguard or without one?"

She sighed and tugged at that wonderfully short skirt. "Go fly your plane. I'm not getting off."

Rudi nodded briskly, careful not to allow any of his triumph to show. He was getting much too good at dissembling. Sometimes it disturbed him, how good he was at it. But not today.

He finished his flight check, radioed the tower and received takeoff clearance. Moments later he was in the air flying west. When he was out of the airport traffic pattern, he engaged the autopilot and stepped back into the small cabin.

"Who's flying the plane?" Ellen looked startled to see him.

"Autopilot. Just long enough for me to get a sandwich and some coffee." Rudi poured from the insulated carafe into his lidded cup. "There is a storm ahead I want to keep an eye on."

"The one past Harrisburg."

"Correct." Rudi winked at her, wondering how much else she'd heard. "I cannot keep anything from you, can I?"

She didn't answer.

He stirred sugar into his coffee and snapped the lid on the cup. "Come up to the cockpit if you like. The view is much better up there."

He picked up a sandwich wrapped in plastic and headed back up front, hoping Ellen would take him up on his invitation. He wanted to talk to her. He would rather have let Samuel stay and do the flying, but he had never allowed anyone to go with him to Buckingham. Until now.

Ellen sat in the soft velour-covered seat staring out the window at fat, fluffy clouds floating past and wondered what in heaven's holy name she was doing in this airplane. She'd been in private corporate jets before, but none so sybaritically luxurious as this one, with the ornate rugs laid over the utilitarian gray carpet and the intricate inlay on the wood-paneled half walls. Nor had she ever been in one alone.

Not that she was exactly alone now. Rudi, her client, the body she was supposed to be guarding rather than lusting after, was on the plane with her. He was just in a separate part of the plane, in the cockpit, flying it. A rich man's self-indulgence, she told herself.

She picked through the lunch basket, mostly to see what was there. She'd been hungry earlier, but no more. Rudi upset her stomach. It couldn't be the combination of guilt, resentment and desire he stirred up in her. But if it was, it was still his fault.

Ellen unwrapped a sandwich and sniffed it. Chicken salad. Very fresh chicken salad. Maybe she could eat a bite or two. She poured a cup of coffee. The first sip set her back on her heels—it was strong enough to stand up and walk out of the cup on its own. But it was good. She added cream and sugar to tone it down a bit, and made up her mind.

Carrying coffee and sandwich, she walked to the cockpit, staggering only once in slight turbulence. Rudi glanced up and smiled when she entered.

"So you decided to come see the cockpit." He gestured at the chair to his right. "Have a seat. Take a look around."

Ellen slid carefully into the seat. She didn't want to touch anything she shouldn't. Her seat had a steering mechanism in front of it that appeared to be locked down. Good. She looked out the window and was mesmerized.

Trees blanketed the rippling ground below them, interspersed with squares and rectangles of bright green or mellow gold, depending, Ellen supposed, on the crops growing there. Blue river ribbons curled through the patchwork, while black roads slashed arrow straight, dotted with fast-moving traffic. And around her—above, below, left, right, before, behind—the sky opened its vast vistas.

She could see clear to tomorrow and back to yesterday. Clouds kept them company like fat, contented sheep. But ahead, a dark line on the horizon shadowed her pleasure in the scene, told her the clouds weren't always contented.

"Is that the storm?" She tipped her head toward it.

"Yes. We will turn south in a few minutes and fly around it." He looked at her. "I do not fly through thunderstorms just to prove how manly I am."

Ellen laughed. "No. You just ride through Central Park on a borrowed horse and snatch women off their feet."

"For fun." A tiny smile tickled the corners of Rudi's lips. "Admit it. It was fun, was it not?"

She shook her head. She might admit it to herself,

but never, ever to him. "You're absolutely outrageous."

"I know." He winked. "And you love it."

Rather than dignify his nonsense with a response, Ellen ate her sandwich.

Before long, they were flying with the dark line of clouds off their right wing, but the storm grew faster than the little jet could fly. The clouds seemed to boil, racing and churning as the pewter-gray froth climbed higher and higher, blotting out the sun. These were angry clouds, throwing lightning back and forth like insults, reaching out to drag Ellen and Rudi into their quarrel.

"Buckle up." Rudi pointed at the shoulder harness attached to Ellen's seat. He already had his fastened, she noticed as she pulled the straps around her and clicked them into place.

"We will get caught in the edges of this storm," he said. "The front is bigger and badder than it looked in the forecast, but we should miss the worst of it."

"Can't we fly above it, or something?" Her hands shook, and she locked them together in her lap. Ellen couldn't believe her nerves were so shot. She'd never had a problem with flying in her life. But then, she'd never been in a plane this small in the middle of a storm that big with her safety in someone else's hands. Her cousin the shrink said she had control issues.

"It is too high. A commercial jetliner would have trouble getting above this one." Rudi shot her a quick smile. "Relax. I have never crashed one yet."

''That's the word that bothers me,'' she muttered.

''What word?''

''Yet.''

Rudi laughed, a big, full-throated sound of pure enjoyment. Then the plane plunged, caught by a sudden downdraft.

Ellen yelped, and Rudi stopped laughing as he wrestled for altitude. The aircraft bucked and jolted like something alive trying to escape a predator's jaws. Ellen squeezed her eyes shut and hung on to the chair's armrests for dear life. She wasn't afraid. But if the plane was going to crash, she didn't want to see it.

Time passed. The jet would level out and climb for a few minutes, then the wind would lash out again with another stomach-floating drop, or a sideways blow, and the struggle would start over. Rudi fought the storm with a fierce light in his eyes that must have been in his ancestors' when they fought the invading Crusaders. Ellen watched him, fascinated.

Except when the downdrafts struck. She couldn't keep her eyes open when the wind pushed the plane toward the ground.

Rain and sleet sporadically battered the little jet. For minutes at a time they would break into the clear, only to have the storm reach out and snare them again. It exhausted Ellen, and she was merely a passenger. She didn't want to think how tired Rudi must be.

Finally, finally the clouds thinned, then dissipated, and nothing shone ahead of them but blue sky.

Rudi took a deep breath and got on the radio. Ellen's ear had been well tuned to pick up the hissing, staticky tones of speech over the airwaves, but pilot talk was full of jargon she didn't know. She understood the English words, the ones like *heading* and *southwest*. The rest of it was beyond her.

"Clear skies ahead," Rudi said when he hung up the microphone. "All the way to California, if we like, according to the weather wizards."

"I guess they'd know." She gave him a lowering look. "We are *not* going to California." It was not a question. Nor was it an option.

Rudi grinned. "No, we are not going to California."

"So where are we going?"

"Not California."

Ellen ground her teeth, then made herself stop. Her doctor blamed the habit for her headaches. "Stop being coy. It doesn't suit you. Where are we going?"

"You will know when we get there. Let it be a surprise. And I am never coy."

"I hate surprises. I'm responsible for your safety. What if these terrorists are waiting for you on the other end of this flight?"

"They are not."

"How do you know?"

"Because even if they knew where we are going, which they do not, they have had insufficient time to get there. And even if they are there, which they are not, they will stand out like a goat in the parlor. You would spot them in five seconds or less."

Ellen scowled at him. "Why won't you tell me

where we're going? And you're about as coy as it's possible for a man to be.''

''Not coy. Clever.'' Rudi winked.

''Rudi—'' She put a threat in her voice. It didn't work.

''Yes, Ellen?'' His smile was inoffensive.

''You're ticking me off. So if you're not telling me because you don't want to make me mad, it's too late. I'm already there. Where are we going?'' She punctuated the words with silence. She locked her hands around the armrests to remind herself that, as much as she wanted to, she couldn't strangle him.

''Our destination is a surprise.''

That again. ''I really hate surprises. They always jump up and bite you in the ass.'' Ellen glowered out the windshield.

''Some surprises are nice. This one is.''

She didn't believe a word of it.

''And if I cannot be coy, you cannot be sullen,'' he added.

''I'm not sullen.'' Her glare should have singed his ears, if there was any justice in the world.

''Right.'' Rudi's smug smile shoved her irritation higher.

Ellen needed to get away, out of the same room with him, lest she lose her marginal grip on her self-control and do something best left unthought of. He was flying the plane, after all.

She fought her way out of the seat belt. ''I'm going to the little girls' room,'' she said. *Before I smack you.*

''All the way aft.'' Rudi glanced up at her, and for

a minute Ellen thought he would say something smart-ass, something that would drive her right off the deep end.

He didn't. "Why do you not take two of the chairs in the cabin and stretch out? You look as if you fought the storm to a standstill single-handedly. You should get some rest."

She didn't know whether to feel insulted because he implied she looked awful or comforted because he showed concern for her well-being. Either one wasn't what she'd expected from a rich, irresponsible, play-boy younger son. But then Rudi had been confounding her expectations from the minute she'd met him.

"Aren't you tired?" she asked.

"I am flying." He grinned. "Besides, it is harder to be a passenger than a pilot coming through a storm. When you are doing the flying, you are taking action. You are in control. Not wincing and ducking and closing your eyes. Not that you did any of those things, of course."

Ellen stood up and stepped out the cockpit door to escape the blasted man, then turned back. "I closed my eyes," she said. She believed in owning up to the truth. "And I really, *really* hate surprises."

When Ellen did not come back to the cockpit, Rudi put the plane on autopilot just long enough to check on her. He found her asleep in the cabin. She sat tipped against the wall in a corner, rather than stretched out as Rudi had suggested. Probably because he had suggested it.

Or maybe she had told herself she would just sit

and look out the window a minute, never intending to fall asleep. That would be like her, from the little Rudi knew of her thus far. She refused to be pushed, didn't like to be led and fought to keep control of everything around her, holding it clutched tight in those long, elegant fingers. But sometimes, apparently, her body overruled her.

Rudi indulged himself with one more look at those slender, forever legs before stepping back into the cockpit. Sleep was good, he thought as he buckled himself back in and flipped the switch to manual. She needed it. Besides that, if she slept long enough, she would not give him trouble over their destination.

At least, not until they landed. Rudi was a great believer in putting off trouble as long as possible.

The storm had delayed them. Enough to make Rudi push the plane a little harder than he liked. If he did not reach the landing strip before dark, they would have to go miles out of the way to a lighted airport. Fortunately it was summer, and the sun stayed above the horizon well into the evening hours. Crossing two time zones helped, also.

The sun was low on the horizon when he spotted the notched bluff just past the rusty smear of river bottom. He aimed for the notch and five minutes later he was over the runway, the wind sock indicating a strong south wind, as usual. Grateful he did not have to land facing the sun's dying glare, Rudi circled the field and put the jet on the asphalt strip with only two or three hard bounces. Not the best runway in the world, especially when the cows strayed across it.

Before he could taxi down the runway to the hangar, Ellen burst into the cockpit.

"Where's the exit?" She knelt to unbuckle his seat harness. "Stop messing around trying to fix things and get out of there."

"What are you doing, woman?"

Distracted by her hands playing in his lap, Rudi drifted slightly off course and ran over something left too near the runway, causing the jet to bump slightly. Ellen clutched at him, one arm locking around his thigh to keep from losing her balance. Rudi would have smacked the plane into the side of the hangar if he had not managed to hit the brakes hard enough to stop it.

"Ellen." He pushed her gently to the other chair. "Wait until the plane stops before you start grabbing the pilot's legs. Let me get the plane in the hangar, and then you may play with my legs all you want, all right?"

She peered out the windscreen, her slender neck swiveling as she checked out her surroundings. Her nostrils flared, subtly surveying the air, perhaps for the scent of smoke. Then her eyes narrowed into anger, and she sank into the copilot's chair.

"The way you landed this thing, throwing me clean out of my seat, how was I supposed to know we didn't crash?" Ellen looked out the window on her side, toward the pink-and-orange sky where the sun had just vanished beyond the distant horizon, then aimed her glare at Rudi again. "It's sunset. You said we'd be back in the city tonight."

He brought the plane to a halt inside the open hangar. "I never said that." He had been very careful not to.

"Okay, you let me assume it."

Before he could inform her that her assumptions were not his responsibility, she had moved on.

"Just where are we, anyway?"

"My place." Rudi shut everything down, then ran the checklist to be sure. "I could not carry you away to the Casbah, but I think this is better."

"You said it was a business meeting." Her eyes flashed fire at him. He'd always thought it a cliché, but she truly was beautiful when she was angry.

"It is. In town, in the morning." He stood and edged between the seats, partially through the door, then offered Ellen his hand. "Coming?"

Rudi held his breath as she looked from his face to his hand and back again, waiting for her to decide. She would come—he had maneuvered her pretty neatly into that. She had to stick with him, at least for now. But would she take his hand? Rudi did not think so. Still, he had to take the chance and offer it.

When her slim, cool fingers slid across his palm and her hand closed around his, the touch jolted him. It sent his persistent awareness of her presence sizzling into raging desire. Every molecule in his body wanted her. Not just for sex, though he could not deny he wanted that, wanted it so much he had to choke off a groan. But he wanted more.

He wanted to see admiration in her eyes. He wanted to hear her laugh. He wanted to argue with her and make up afterward. He wanted to wake up with her in the morning after a night of hot, mindless, slow, sultry sex, and have her smile at him simply because she liked him.

And Rudi knew, somewhere down deep in his gut, that if he rushed the sex, he would never get the smile. It might kill him, but he intended to take his sweet time with this woman.

"Well?" Ellen's voice broke into his musing, and he realized he still stood like a fool in the cockpit doorway holding her hand. "Are we going to get off this airplane any time in this millennium?"

Rudi grinned. He loved her sass. "Come along. Meet the natives."

Four

Ellen let Rudi open the jet's door, but she was the first one through it, her hand on the gun in her purse as she descended the narrow ladderway. The hangar, a primitive construct of corrugated tin, was empty.

She walked to the open entrance and looked out into the blue twilight. Open land stretched out ahead of her, broken only by a flat-topped hill in the far distance. Short, scrubby bushes covered the land, almost silver in the dusky light. The black-topped runway became a dirt road about a mile distant, and looped around to the west, toward high rocky mountains.

Foothills, Ellen corrected herself, seeing the sunset-gilded peaks of higher mountains in the distance beyond. She'd never in all her life seen so much…nothing. Or so few people. Like none, besides herself and Rudi. She would definitely be able to spot a terrorist in this vast wasteland. They'd be the only other people out here.

"Where in the world have you brought me?" she muttered.

"As I said—" Rudi spoke at her elbow "—this is my place."

She looked around at the empty, echoing hangar. "Nice house."

Rudi chuckled. "The house is at the base of that rise." He pointed at one of the hills to the west.

"I'm not exactly dressed for a cross-country hike."

"Do not worry. Our ride is coming."

Just then, Ellen heard the growl of a motor. Headlights pierced the gloom as a pickup truck shouldered up out of a fold in the land she hadn't seen, and rumbled its way onto the runway and up to the hangar. Her grip tightened on the automatic pistol still hidden in her purse, and she stepped in front of Rudi. He might know who the pickup belonged to, but she didn't.

The lanky, grizzled cowboy who unfolded himself from the truck certainly didn't look like a Muslim terrorist, however. Rudi's wide smile as he stepped past her reassured her more.

"Bill." Rudi embraced the man and kissed him on both cheeks.

Bill was still wiping off his cheeks when Rudi drew Ellen forward. "This is Ellen Sheffield. She'll be staying with us for a few days."

"Pleased to meet you, Miss Sheffield." Bill shook

her hand with great ceremony, his hand as dry and callused as old leather. "Welcome to New Mexico."

"I—" She had to pause a moment to digest the knowledge that she was in New Mexico. Rudi would pay for this. He most definitely would pay. "I'm pleased to meet you, Mr...." She paused again, waiting for his response to her prompt.

"Just call me Bill. Everybody else does." Bill reclaimed his hand and turned away.

"I'd be happy to. But I'd still like to know your last name."

Ellen could feel Rudi's silent laughter beside her as Bill turned back, eyebrows climbing his laddered forehead.

"Dadgum, boy," he said in a slow-as-five-o'clock-traffic drawl, "if you were gonna wait so long before bringin' a woman home, don't you think you coulda found one who wasn't so snippy?"

"I'm a bodyguard," Ellen said. "The fact that I'm female is immaterial. And I still don't know your last name."

"It's Chandler." Bill gave her a long, slow, head-to-toe once-over. Ellen endured it, as she had all the others in her life. "And you look pretty durn material to me."

He looked at Rudi. "You bring your usual luggage?"

"Yes." Rudi gently tugged Ellen's hand out of her purse and escorted her to the pickup truck. "Has everything gone well here?"

"Right as rain, except we haven't had any. Rain." Bill got in the driver's side and waited.

Ellen eyed the open passenger door of the pickup in dismay. She'd never been in a truck before, and now she knew why. They were not made to get into while wearing a dress. Particularly not a short, snug dress like the lime-green sheath she presently had on.

"Do you need assistance?" Rudi murmured in her ear.

"No, I—um—" Ellen lifted her foot, but the seams of her skirt popped alarmingly before she could get it high enough to set on the step.

Before she could try something else, Rudi grasped her around the waist and lifted her in, then climbed in after her.

"Thanks, son." Bill started the engine. "I figured we'd be pussyfootin' out here till sunup waiting for Miss Bodyguard to figure out how to get in a truck."

Ellen ignored the old Neanderthal. She'd known a thousand men just like him. He wasn't worth the waste of her time to try to prove him wrong.

"How is the beautiful Annabelle?" Rudi asked.

"Anxious to see you again, but she'll keep till tomorrow. She left you some supper." Bill paused while he drove the truck into a gully and out again. "I reckon there'll be enough for the both of you, even if she was only expecting one."

Annabelle? Ellen refused to give Rudi the satisfaction of looking at him. She refused to play his game. If he kept a woman in his New Mexico hideaway, that was his business. She was just the bodyguard.

"I am desolate," Rudi said. "I am forced to wait until tomorrow to see my Annabelle? How can I eat when I am deprived of her company?"

Bill snorted. "You may think I'm no-count enough that you can flirt with my wife like that, but I'm thinkin' your bodyguard here can straighten you out right fast."

Annabelle was Mrs. Chandler. Ellen caught herself when she heard Rudi's laughter, stopped her glare from shooting at him. She didn't care who Annabelle was. Rudi's flirtations were none of her business. None.

But the shape of the situation shifted again, back to her original assessment of his purpose in bringing her here. Rudi had seduction on his mind.

Well, he could just wipe it right out of there, because Ellen wasn't playing. She was here for one reason and one reason only. To do her job and guard his body.

"How far is it to the house?" she asked.

"Another couple miles," Bill said.

"What kind of security does it have?"

"State of the art." Rudi stretched his arm across the back of the seat, and incidentally around Ellen. Step one of his plan, she was certain. "I do not use motion-sensor sound alarms because of the wildlife, but everything else is installed. Also, the house cannot be approached unseen."

"Good." Ellen nodded her head once, briskly. Keep everything businesslike, and she could keep it under control.

"Relax." Rudi smiled at her. "There is no danger here. Not from terrorists, at any rate."

Ellen shrugged. It was her job to make sure. He was probably right. She couldn't envision terrorists braving this no-man's-land of New Mexico. But it was still her job to stay alert.

She sat up straight in the center of the seat and watched the bushes jolt by, as the truck alternately lurched, crawled and jounced its way along. Rudi's head settled against the back glass of the pickup's cab. When Ellen glanced his way, she saw his mouth had dropped open, and he slept, despite the rattling of his head on the window.

The truck hit a bigger-than-usual rock, and Rudi's head bounced hard. He blinked awake and pulled his arm in, straightening slightly on the seat, as if determined to stay awake. But in seconds his eyes shut again, and his head fell back on the window as he slumped low in the seat.

Ellen sighed. It was a conspiracy. The whole world conspired against her, forcing her into niceness. She was not a nice person. She didn't want to be a nice person. Nice people got dumped on.

And yet. Ellen found herself tipping Rudi's head forward, off the back glass, and sideways. Against her shoulder. She hoped he didn't drool in his sleep. If he drooled, the niceness was over.

Bill was apparently as taciturn as cowboys were reputed to be. The remainder of the trip passed in silence, except for the roar of the motor and the occasional very soft snore from Rudi.

The sky had darkened to a deep navy blue just a shade lighter than the black horizon and stars were beginning to appear when the truck heaved itself up onto an almost-paved road and turned left. The surface was graded and graveled, and much smoother than the rutted track they'd just left. A few minutes later, lights winked on, triggered by motion sensors, illuminating what Ellen guessed to be some dozen acres. Rudi's house sat in the center of the light pool.

Ellen stared. This was no little cabin in the foot-hills. This was the Ponderosa. It was Tara. Manderley. A house like this deserved a name. Half log cabin, half glass palace, it nestled into the rocks jutting from the hill behind as if it grew out of them. It belonged in this wild place, and yet, somehow, it promised lux-uries beyond Ellen's most fantastic dreams. And she could dream some pretty big fantasies.

Bill pulled the pickup to a halt in front of the wide stairway leading up to the entry deck. Rudi jolted awake, springing upright before he blinked. Ellen brushed off her shoulder, brushing away the touch of his head.

"We're here," Bill said. "You need anything else?"

"No. Thank you." Rudi opened the pickup door and slid out, stumbling once before his knees caught and held. He turned and offered his hand to Ellen.

She ignored it, preferring to rely on herself, to by-pass his little courtesies. They were all part of the web he tried to weave, a web she had no intention of getting caught in. In fact, she was no slouch at weav-ing her own webs, which was how she came to know all about them.

"Your keys are in the usual spot," Bill said through the still-open truck door. "She's gassed up and serviced. Ready to roll."

"Thank you, Bill. I will see you tomorrow, then."

Rudi shut the door, and Bill and his pickup rumbled off.

Rudi gave Ellen a little bow and gestured toward the stairs. "Shall we go in?"

Scowling, Ellen started up. "Who knows you're here?"

"Besides my family and the Chandlers?" Rudi climbed the few steps at her side, and led the way across the broad deck to the front door. He unlocked the door. "Only your office, of course."

Ellen didn't bother answering. She reached inside and flipped on the interior light, the gun out of her handbag and in her hand this time, as she stepped into Rudi's house.

She could see almost all of the lower level from the door. A massive native-stone fireplace rose on the north wall. The kitchen, with cabinets matching the unstained pine log walls, took up part of the western side of the house, and Ellen surmised that a bedroom or two lay beyond the doorway on the south wall. A stairway made of split logs suspended from yet more logs rose from near the middle of the room's expanse, leading to a loft above, and possibly more bedrooms. Comfortable, masculine, rustic furniture divided the vast open space into areas for dining, relaxing and conversing according to its placement.

Quickly Ellen checked the rooms she couldn't see into, locating a luxurious master bedroom and bath complete with whirlpool on the first floor, and four more bedrooms upstairs beyond the loft area. Decks surrounded the house, void of occupants save for an annoyed squirrel. Ellen lifted the cover off the hot tub on the deck outside the main bedroom, just to be sure.

"Are we safe?" Rudi asked, a smile curving his lips as he pulled a casserole dish from the oven.

"For now." Ellen put her weapon away. She had to smile herself at the picture he made. "You look real cute wearing that oven mitt. Real natural."

"Why, thank you." Again he made that little flourishing bow, still holding the hot dish.

Ellen wished she had said nothing, hadn't even noticed. The oven mitt somehow emphasized his exotic masculinity, the breadth of his shoulders and strength of his arms. Didn't the man own a shirt in the right size? Surely he could find something that didn't strain at the seams.

Rudi set the dish on the table. "Are you hungry?"

"I guess." Ellen shrugged. "What is there to eat?"

Steam rose, redolent of tomatoes and spices and things Mexican, as he peeled away the foil. "I do not know the name of it, but I assure you, it is delicious. Annabelle could cook a sow's ear and make it delicious."

"Just who are Bill and Annabelle?" Ellen asked, opening kitchen drawers at random, hunting silverware.

"Sit down." Rudi took her by both arms, turned her toward the table and gave her a gentle push. "You are my guest. I will take care of everything."

This was a new kind of seduction scene, watching a man wait on her with his own hands, rather than snapping fingers at a restaurant waiter. She kind of liked it. Not that it would work.

Rudi set a plate in front of her, creamy blue-painted stoneware. Then he set a napkin, cloth, in the middle of the plate and a fork, real silver, on top of the napkin.

"We do not need knives for this," he muttered as he collected wineglasses from where they hung upside down on a rack. He rinsed them out and dried them quickly before setting one at each place. Instead of wine, he pulled two amber bottles from the refrigerator.

The label was unfamiliar to Ellen, unreadable. "What is this?"

"Beer." Rudi found a serving spoon and stabbed it into the casserole. "Mexican beer for the Mexican food. I learned to appreciate it when I was at university." He surveyed the table. "Do you need anything else?"

Ellen shrugged, hiding her pleasure at being asked. Rudi sat down in the chair beside her, at the place he had prepared. He opened his beer, poured it into the glass, then held it up in a toast. "Drink with me."

She drank straight from the mouth of her bottle, then held it out to answer his toast. "What are we drinking to?"

She knew, of course. The toast would be to her, or to both of them, or to beautiful women. But it would be about sex and seduction.

Rudi's perfect mouth curved in that perfect smile. "To conversation," he said.

Conversation? Ellen blinked and belatedly tipped her bottle up to her mouth. Damn the man for being able to confuse her. Again.

Maybe that was how he planned to seduce her. Get her all confused until she didn't know which way was up, then pounce when she was helpless. Well, Ellen Sheffield was never helpless. Ever. But she was definitely confused.

Rudi served Ellen's plate with the food Annabelle had prepared for them, and then served his own.

"Eat." He picked up his fork. "I promise you, it is not poisoned or otherwise tampered with." He took a bite, hissing faintly as the fire of the peppers hidden in the meat hit his palate. "It may be a trifle spicy, however."

He could not resist chuckling at Ellen's suspicious expression as she poked at the cheese and tortillas.

"You never did answer my question." She finally stopped poking and took a bite.

Rudi could tell when the peppers hit, but only because tears started in the corners of her eyes. She disguised the rest of her reaction, reaching casually for the beer as if flames were not about to shoot from her ears.

"Is it hot?" he asked.

"Not at all." She cleared her throat, obviously unwilling to either choke or cough. "Bill and Annabelle—who are they?"

"Bill manages the property. And Annabelle cares for the house, and for me when I am here." Rudi smiled.

He found one of the sliced jalapeños and deliberately, making sure Ellen saw him, stabbed it with his fork and carried it to his mouth, where it quickly reminded him why he usually left the peppers sitting on the rim of his plate. He shoveled in a big mouthful of starchy tortillas and beans immediately after the pepper, to dilute some of the burn.

"Do you like it?" he asked, pointing at the food on Ellen's plate.

"Delicious." She blinked back tears.

"If the peppers are too hot, just leave them on the side of your plate." Rudi uncovered another and ate it, even as his conscience and his tongue chided him for his wickedness. "Sometimes women find them more than they can handle."

"No, they're not too hot. They're good." Ellen took his dare, snaring a pepper from her own plate and popping it into her mouth, where she swallowed it virtually whole.

Rudi, Rudi, you are an evil man. And he ate another, hoping his digestion could stand up to the assault.

"So, Ellen, now that we can finally have that talk you promised..." He paused to smile, hoping it looked as guileless as he wished it to. "Tell me about yourself. Have you family?"

"And then some." She looked up from her plate where she had been stirring and gave him a shy smile that jolted him clear to his toes. "Although I guess I can't complain. I only have half as many brothers as you do."

"Only four brothers, then. Allah is indeed merciful to you." He grinned, and she laughed. "Are they older or younger than you?"

"I'm the middle child, unfortunately." She sighed.

"Usually it's the middle child who feels invisible, but being the only girl, I wasn't so lucky."

"Be glad you were not. Invisible is not a pleasant thing to be." As Rudi well knew. Being number seven among nine brothers was about as invisible as a boy could get.

"I can't believe you've ever felt invisible," Ellen said. "Not the way your family comes unglued when you're not where you're supposed to be."

"Ah, but there is invisible, as in unseen, and there is invisible, as in seeing only what the viewer wishes to see. I have always been seen as no more than a copy of my brothers. A body to fill in the gap between Hamid and Ahmed."

Why was he telling her this? He had intended to pry out Ellen's secrets, not lay his own out for view, as if asking for her pity. Angry with himself, he stabbed the pepper he had just uncovered and ate it, enjoying the burn.

"Actually," Ellen said, toying with a shred of meat, "I think I do know about that kind of invisible."

Rudi's eyebrows went up, his gaze fastened on her, as his internal detector of secrets signaled wildly. "Because you were the only girl and everyone expected you to be sweet and feminine?"

Ellen looked at him, surprise in her expression. Then she threw her head back and laughed, a full-hearted, joyous laugh such as he had not heard from anyone in too long, and never from Ellen. It was possible she frequently laughed this way, and Rudi had simply not been near her enough to know it, but he did not think so.

"No," she said, wiping her eyes as she took another bite.

Rudi noticed she left the jalapeño on the plate. Then she noticed that he noticed, and she oh-so-casually scooped it up and ate it, coughing only once.

"No," she repeated. "I did everything my brothers did, from baseball to ice hockey. And if anyone tried to tell me I couldn't, I knocked him down.

"Oh, I had Barbie dolls and Wonder Woman boots, but my Barbie dolls went out on bivouac with Steve's G.I. Joes—Steve is my next younger brother—and got blown to smithereens with Roger's firecrackers. Roger is the oldest. We had to steal his firecrackers because we were too young to have any of our own."

Rudi liked this side of her, wanted to know all of it. "Tell me more. Tell me about the Wonder Woman boots."

Ellen's eyes grew wistful. "I loved those boots. I got them for Christmas when I was six, I think. And I wore those boots everywhere, until I outgrew them. Even to school if Mom didn't catch me. I had Danny's old Superman cape. Danny comes between me and Roger. I wore the cape pretty much everywhere, too. Until Danny convinced me I could fly in it."

"He what?" Rudi sat up straight, alarmed. But she must have come to no harm from it, for she sat here before him eating Annabelle's delicious fiery food.

"Well, he didn't really convince me." Ellen's fond chuckle did not do much to reassure Rudi. "I was

pretty sure the cape didn't have any Superman pow-
ers. That's why I didn't jump off the roof.''

''Thank goodness.'' Rudi almost collapsed in his
chair as the relief rushed through him.

''I just jumped out of my second-story bedroom
window.''

''What?'' His heart could not take this jolting.
''You jumped from a second-story window thinking
you could fly because of a stupid red cape?''

Ellen laughed, a gleeful chortle this time. ''Don't
forget the boots. The boots were supposed to be these
superpowered pogo-stick things. Like landing on a
trampoline. If I didn't fly, I'd just jump right back to
the window.''

''What possessed you to do such a foolish thing?''

''He dared me.'' Ellen shrugged. ''Don't tell me
you never did anything like that, because I won't believe you.''

''I never jumped off a roof.''

She lifted one skeptical eyebrow.

''Or out of a window.''

Her other eyebrow went up. Rudi resisted that cool
appraisal for approximately ten seconds before he
broke.

''Oh, very well. I once tried to dive to the bottom
of the pond in our garden because Fahdlan told me
Aladdin's lamp was hidden there. But the pond was
only four feet deep.''

''How old were you?''

''Four years old. However, I remember it very
well.''

"And who had to haul you out when you almost drowned?"

Rudi shot her a sharp glance. How had she known that? "My brother Ibrahim. And how many bones did you break in your brave leap into the sky?"

"Only two." She grimaced. "Both arms. Danny had to feed me till the casts came off. His punishment for daring me to jump. And mine."

"Do you always accept dares?"

Ellen held his gaze a moment, then she speared a jalapeño, put it in her mouth and chewed very slowly. Tears again gathered in the corners of her eyes, and she had to clear her throat before she swallowed. Rudi watched her throat work, wishing he could kiss his way along the path the pepper took.

"Always," she said.

Rudi had to clear his own throat and remind himself what her word referred to. "I shall have to remember that, if there is something in particular I wish you to do."

He licked his lips and noticed Ellen watching his tongue travel across his mouth. Then she copied the action, and he could only stare at her tongue darting out and across her lips. What madness had possessed him to bring her here?

That madness, obviously, but had he been required to give in to it? Too late to change anything now. Impulse had carried him into deep waters once more.

And he did not know whether, this time, he could get himself out again.

Five

Ellen stared into Rudi's deep, soulful, melting, coffee-brown eyes, framed by the thickest, curliest lashes that no man had any right to possess. What had he just said? Something about things he wanted her to do?

He licked his lips again, and again Ellen fought the tingle at the back of her neck as his tongue traveled across those eminently kissable lips. They parted.

And Ellen caught herself before she leaned toward them.

What was wrong with her? She had to be in control of this little seduction scene, had to keep him off balance and slavering, ready to do whatever she wanted. So how did she wind up being the one off balance?

She glanced down at her plate, intending to distract herself with food, and discovered that some gremlin had climbed onto the table and eaten everything on her plate when she wasn't looking.

"Would you like more?" Rudi asked, his hand on the serving spoon.

Ellen looked at him and almost lost herself in those dark eyes again. She could not do that. Not ever again.

"Much as I've enjoyed our little pepper-eating contest," she said, "I think I've had enough. Which bedroom is mine?"

"Take this one." Rudi gestured toward the first-floor suite.

Ellen's eyes narrowed. "And where, pray tell, will you be sleeping?"

"There are many rooms in this house." He stood and took her hand as she rose, despite her effort to avoid his grasp. "I will have no trouble in finding a place to sleep."

"I don't want to take your room." She let him draw her toward the bedroom door, but stalled outside it.

"My guest should have the best my home has to offer."

"What about the dishes?" Ellen turned back to the kitchen. Rudi stopped her before she could take a step.

"Annabelle will wash them when she comes in the morning. I will put away the remaining food. You are my guest. Please…" He opened the bedroom door and indicated with a graceful wave that she should enter.

"I really don't think—"

"But I do," Rudi interrupted. "If you are going to begin talking about bodyguarding and employment, perhaps I should point out that you will be closer to the entrances by sleeping here on the first floor."

"There is that."

"Please. Humor me."

The mere fact that he wanted so badly for her to stay in the master bedroom ought to be reason enough for Ellen to insist on another room. But she found herself nodding in agreement. "Oh, all right. If you're going to be that way about it."

"I am." He smiled at her. One of his patented smiles that could put furnace companies out of business, the way it seemed to raise the ambient temperature. "I will be sleeping in the bedroom right at the top of the stairs."

She shot him a suspicious glare.

He chuckled. "I assumed you would want to know which room I would take in order to better perform your guarding tasks. To be sure no one creeps in during the night to slit my throat."

He drew his finger across his throat, drawing her eye to it. Strong, muscular, shadowed with the day's beard, and yet vulnerable, his throat matched the rest of Rudi. Ellen told herself firmly that she did not want to press her lips to the faint pulse she saw there.

Rudi leaned toward her.

Here it comes, the kiss that's supposed to knock my socks off and convince me to share the room with him. Trouble was, Ellen was afraid Rudi's kiss really would knock her socks off. But she refused to run away from it.

Then he bypassed her mouth and pressed a warm, dry kiss on her forehead. "Sleep well, my dear Ellen."

He turned away, leaving her staring gape mouthed at him.

Damn him! She whirled away and slammed the door shut. She could hear him laughing through the closed door and wanted to open it again and yank out a few handfuls of that black, silky hair. How could he do this to her?

Not "how could he" as in how did he dare, but "how could he" as in how in the world *did* he do it?

Ellen knew men. She knew what they wanted, what turned them on and what made them angry. She knew how to push all the right buttons to make a man do what she wanted him to do. She'd learned it well, after Davis. Never had any man been able to push her buttons in return. Until now.

Rudi didn't behave the way she expected. At virtually every turn he surprised her. He was different.

And that was how he had stolen control away from her. She had no set of instructions for dealing with a man like Rudi, no experience in handling a man who would kiss her forehead at his own bedroom door and walk away, leaving her to sleep alone, without even attempting to join her. That innocent kiss had left her tingling and wanting, more than any tongue fight ever had.

She was going to have to play this one by ear, and when it came to Rudi, Ellen feared she was tone-deaf.

The big black SUV turned headfirst into a parking place on the downtown street—the only downtown street—of Buckingham, New Mexico. Ellen stepped out onto the red brick pavement, adjusting her sunglasses against the brightness of the summer sun.

It seemed harsher here, more glaring than she remembered it being in New York. Maybe because of the altitude, considerably above New York's sea level. Or maybe the sun had no pollution to cut through here. Whatever the reason, Ellen's stylish half-tint designer shades did not suffice to cut the brilliance.

She hitched up her borrowed jeans, which had been left in her bedroom before she woke by the efficient and estimable Annabelle, and stepped up the knee-high curb onto the sidewalk. The jeans bothered her. Not because they threatened to slip off her hips and tangle around her knees with every step, but because someone had entered the house, entered the *bedroom* where she slept, and she hadn't known it.

Just because she'd woken twice in the night, terrified by dreams that she'd gone deaf, and then been unable to go back to sleep was no excuse for screwing up. It was her job to be alert at all times. Still, she would never complain about New York City traffic noise again.

"When is this meeting?" she asked Rudi as he joined her on the sidewalk.

He checked his watch. "Eleven o'clock."

"So we have a little time before then." Ellen hoisted the jeans again.

"Yes. Was there something you wished to do?"

His mouth ought to be declared a controlled substance, Ellen thought. It was definitely addictive. She couldn't stop staring at it, wanting to taste. But she forced herself.

Blinking helped. So did looking past his shoulder when she talked to him. She was a protector. She had to keep an eye out for bad guys, not go comatose staring at her protectee.

"If there's anything in this grand metropolis resembling a department store," she said, "I thought I might find something to wear that would stay on."

"That would be a pity." Rudi's voice sounded so sincerely solemn that Ellen risked looking at him. The mischief shining in his big brown eyes made her want to smack him. Not good bodyguard behavior.

"And why is that?" The words grated out between her teeth.

"I was so looking forward to spending the day waiting—perhaps hoping—that Annabelle's clothes would *not* stay on."

She couldn't smack him, but she could at least glare.

Rudi's smile stayed where it was, and he pointed down the street. "I believe there is a store that will have what you are seeking. There are things in the display window other than clothing, but I remember seeing clothing as well."

Saye's was a mix of antiques, gifts and clothes, which would have charmed Ellen if she'd encountered it in New York. Or anywhere that she could go to another store and buy normal clothes. All this store carried was tight jeans in every shade that denim could be dyed, and shirts to match.

The jeans wouldn't be so bad, Ellen decided, if she could find a shirt without a pointed yoke or pearl snaps. The ones without snaps had cute embroidered flowers or teddy bears on them. Ellen did not do cute.

Finally she bought two pairs of jeans that actually fit. Two, because Rudi had told her they'd be in New Mexico at least one more day. She had the store owner put one pair in the sack with the sleeveless, disgustingly cute teddy-bear-print shirt, and she wore the red-checked-gingham, pearl-snapped shirt out of the store with the other pair of jeans. Rudi owed her big time. Making him pay for the clothes was only the beginning. She intended to collect a piece of his hide.

"You look very nice," he said as he followed her out the door.

"I look like Daisy Mae Clampett," she retorted, slapping him in the chest with the sack. "I look like an idiot."

Taking the sack from her, Rudi looked her over, head to toe. This once-over felt different from the others she'd endured. Everywhere his gaze touched she tingled. She wanted to snarl at him, tell him to take his roving eye off her or she would remove it for him. But she couldn't. He'd frozen the words right in her throat with his looking. Or maybe he'd burned them to ashes.

His gaze caressed her, warmed her inside. Good Lord, her nipples were getting hard. Thank God for Victoria and the secrets her bras could hide. This settled it. Ellen was going to see Cousin Alice the shrink the minute she got home. She had gone completely over the edge into lunacy.

"The shoes," Rudi said, startling Ellen out of her appalled reverie.

"What?" Her thoughts were still scattered, and she'd lost the broom to sweep them together again.

"Your shoes do not go with the rest of your clothing." Rudi nodded, as if he'd just solved the secrets of the universe.

"Yeah, I realize that high-heeled sandals don't exactly go with gingham." Her voice carried all the disdain she felt for the word. *Gingham.* Even the sound of it made her shudder. "But I didn't see any saddle oxfords around."

"Boots," Rudi said.

She lifted an eyebrow and tilted her head. He was nuttier than she was. "Are you on some kind of quota system? Did somebody ration your words so you have to save them up because you'll run out if you use too many words at once?"

Rudi laughed, so handsome in the sunlight with the mountains as his backdrop that Ellen's stomach curled around, kicked her heart into pounding and jolted something loose lower down that started to purr.

"You need some boots," he said, offering his arm. "I will buy you a pair of boots, and this afternoon we can go riding."

"I don't ride." Reluctantly she slipped her hand into the crook of his elbow, unable to keep from it, unable to resist his charm or that stupid perfect smile.

"Does that mean you never have, or you never

wish to?'' Rudi started down the street, the breeze off the mountains stirring his sable curls.

''It means I don't know how.'' Nor was she sure she wanted to know, but she wouldn't say that out loud.

''That can be remedied. Riding is not a difficult thing to learn, if one merely wishes to ride for one's own pleasure.'' He paused, walking in silence for a moment as if absorbed in thought. ''Unless, of course, one is afraid of horses.''

There he went, pushing her buttons again. ''I'm not afraid of horses or anything else.''

''Then it is settled. I will buy you boots, and this afternoon we will ride.''

''In the open? I don't think so.''

''We are in the open now.''

''Yes, and the back of my neck is crawling from all the eyes on us.'' Ellen surveyed their surroundings, but saw nothing out of the ordinary. The few people on the street wore their jeans and boots like second skins, smiled and nodded. Not exactly terrorist behavior.

''You know how remote my home is. The area I will take you to ride is even more remote. No one will be able to reach it without your notice.'' He opened the door to a store with a neon boot in the window and Ellen went in, grumbling.

''I still don't like it,'' she said.

''You will like it once you are on your horse.'' Rudi turned his perfect smile on the salesclerk, a woman somewhere between thirty-five and sixty, with weathered skin that had Ellen wishing she'd been more generous with the sunscreen that morning.

Rudi's smile had its usual effect, and in fifteen minutes Ellen was equipped with a pair of black cowboy boots with fancy red stitching on the tops and extra socks to wear with them. She felt almost like a little girl again, playing dress-up. The boots fulfilled a secret fantasy she'd never known she had.

Then the salesclerk rattled off the total.

Ellen closed her gaping mouth, grabbed Rudi's arm and spun him around as she simultaneously tried to remove the boots from her feet. "I'm not doing this," she said. "That's too much. I can't let you pay—"

"Yes, you can." Rudi pulled a wad of cash big enough to choke an elephant from his pocket and peeled off several bills. Ellen grabbed at his hand, trying to stop him from giving them to the clerk, but with one foot half out of her boot, she nearly toppled. Rudi caught her arm, supporting her and holding her at bay while he handed the money to the clerk.

"Rudi," Ellen whispered. "I can't accept these. They're too expensive."

"If I bought you jewelry as a gift," he said, "I would spend three times the amount. This is a small thing. You can accept the boots, and you will."

"But—"

He cut off her protest. "You cannot ride a horse wearing sandals, nor can you accompany me this afternoon unless you are on horseback. If you do not go with me, I will go alone."

Rudi knelt before her and tugged the boot back on her foot, then looked up at her from that position as he smoothed her jeans down over the boot top. He spoke, his voice bedroom soft, so that only Ellen could hear him, despite the fascinated clerk holding out his change. "If you must, think of this as a business requirement, a purchase necessary to fulfill your employment obligations."

His fingers tickled the back of her knee, and the knee almost buckled. Rudi was stirring up things she'd rather he left alone, making her want things that weren't possible.

"But," he said as he rose to his feet, "know that this gift has nothing to do with business. It is for you, and you alone."

She knew it. That was why she couldn't take them. But if she didn't have the boots, she couldn't ride. Why did he have to do these things to her?

Rudi collected his change and escorted her out of the store, Ellen walking awkwardly beside him. The soles of the boots were slick and stiff, and the heels lower than she was used to. The fit was different, changing her walk. It would be a while before she felt comfortable in her new cowboy boots.

Five minutes later they reached a vacant lot across from the Buckingham schools. Pipe, heavy machinery and unidentified metal parts lay scattered all over the lot in a semblance of order, though Ellen couldn't say what that order might be. In the center of the lot a small derrick sat silent. It looked just like the ones she'd seen in movies, only smaller.

Rudi shook hands with the men waiting there and put on the hard hat they gave him. There was a brief scramble while another hat was found for Ellen, and the meeting in and around the machinery began.

She stood back and played bodyguard, ignoring the curious and speculative glances sent her way. In a few minutes the men got involved in their discussion and mostly forgot her presence. Ellen listened, as she usually did on this kind of assignment.

"We've gone down a thousand feet and still have nothing but dry hole," the short, thickset man said.

"How is the water situation, Mayor?" Rudi asked.

The mayor, a white-haired, red-faced cowboy, thought a moment before speaking. "Not good. We're having to get people to fill up their bathtubs in the morning so they'll have water in the evening when the pressure's down. We've been buying from some of the other towns around, but they're in trouble, too, it's been so long since we've had any rain to speak of. And we can't afford to keep drilling if there's nothing down there."

"The water is there," Rudi said. "I am sure of it. I have studied all of the information many times. It is there, but it is deep."

"We can't afford—" the mayor began, but Rudi waved him off.

"Do not worry about the cost. Keep drilling. I will pay."

"I don't feel quite right about that." The mayor rubbed the back of his neck. "You already did the geological study for nothing, helped us pick the site and bought the land to drill on."

Rudi gestured him to silence again. "I am a part of this community. If I can help, I must. The cost is unimportant. A thousand feet more. If you do not reach water at two thousand feet, notify me, and we can consider then what steps to take."

Ellen watched Rudi discuss the drilling with the foreman, and followed him around the well site, revising her opinion of him with every step she took. This meeting wasn't to impress her. Rudi had already been on his way here when he swept her onto that horse in Central Park. Except for glancing at her regularly, as if to make sure she was still present, Rudi devoted his attention to business.

This was the real Rudi. Caring, generous, capable. She'd been attracted to him from the beginning, had even liked him. The flight to Buckingham had given her respect for his flying skills, and now she'd found other things to respect and admire him for. Maybe he was more different from the men she knew than she'd realized.

That thought made her very uneasy, because it made her like him even more, and that could be dangerous. She could not afford to let her guard down. Not the one that protected Rudi, and especially not the one that protected herself.

Rudi allowed his horse to dawdle a few paces so he could watch his companion. No. Admit it, his conscience prodded. You encouraged your horse to fall back. But the sight was well worth it.

Strands of long golden hair had escaped from Ellen's ponytail and floated about her face in the breeze. Her hips swayed with the motion of her horse, making it difficult for Rudi to ride comfortably as he watched her. But he could not tear his gaze away.

He wanted her. He had from the very beginning, but if this time alone together passed with nothing more than a kiss...

He would not be satisfied. Far from it. His frustration would reach unmeasured heights. But already he felt that the trip had accomplished its purpose.

Rudi had begun to see the Ellen behind that polished facade, the little girl who would accept any dare to prove herself. She still refused to back down from any challenge, but he sensed something more. Something that would explain the mask she hid behind. Something she would not easily reveal.

Ellen twisted in the saddle and smiled at him, open and friendly. "What are you doing messing around back there? Get up here and tell me what I'm looking at."

Rudi laughed and urged his mount alongside hers. "Land," he said, sweeping his arm across the horizon. "Trees. Rocks. And there—" He pointed as he spotted them. "Antelope."

"Where?" Ellen stretched, standing slightly in her stirrups as she looked. "I don't see—"

"There." Rudi touched her shoulder and directed her gaze. "You are searching too far. They are closer."

"Practically under my nose." Her voice softened when she saw them. "They're beautiful. They almost look painted, with those striped faces."

Rudi watched the brown-and-white animals grazing on the hillside, their short, straight, single-spike antlers dull in the bright light. "They remind me of the gazelles I sometimes saw at home."

"Gazelles? In the desert?"

"At the oases. Qarif is on the coast. More rocks than sand." Rudi surveyed the stark, beautiful landscape around them for a moment. "This reminds me of Qarif to some degree. There is no ocean nearby, of course, but water is the same precious treasure in both places. And in both places, there is more rock than soil."

"And there are antelopes," Ellen said.

"Yes." Rudi smiled. She understood.

"So where are we going?" She scanned the terrain with that radar-beam gaze of hers.

"This way."

Ellen caught him off guard when she hauled her horse to a stop and glared at him. "That's it," she snapped. "I have had all I can take of your cryptic half-truths. You tell me right now where we are going, or I'm knocking your sorry butt off that horse and hauling you back to town. And I don't mean Buckingham."

Rudi blinked at her, surprised by her outburst. But then, why should he be? He had not been truthful with her from the beginning, still was not, and he well knew Ellen did not possess large amounts of patience.

"My apologies," he said. "I have no definite destination. I merely thought that we might ride into the hills where there are trees. I did not intend to be cryptic."

Ellen continued to glower at him.

"And my butt is not sorry," he added. "I have

been told that it is—'' He broke off, as if trying to remember. ''Ah, yes. That it is mighty fine.''

She snorted. With laughter, he hoped.

''What's over there?''

Rudi accepted the change of topic and looked where she pointed, at a low, steep rock face rising sharply from a dry wash. ''A small canyon begins just past that face. I should have cattle grazing in the meadow there.''

His horse stirred, and Rudi brought it easily under control. ''Sometimes I climb to the top of the cliff and watch them.''

''You do not.'' Her retort was instantaneous.

''I do not climb the face, or I do not watch the cows?''

''Either. Both.''

She no longer scowled, but Rudi liked her skepticism even less. She maligned his manhood. ''I have climbed that rock face a dozen times.''

''Yeah, right.'' Ellen actually scoffed.

Rudi wondered how he could wish so strongly to strangle her and to kiss her at the same moment. Fury swallowed up his words, bound his hands. She was fortunate.

''Anyway,'' she said, ''if you did climb it a dozen times, it's probably no big deal. I bet a baby could climb that. A baby still in diapers.''

''You could not climb it.'' He found his voice.

''If you can climb it, I can climb it,'' she sneered.

''You cannot. Not without asking for help.''

''I don't need anybody's help to climb those rocks.''

"Prove it." Rudi reined his prancing mount in a tight circle.

"You prove it first."

"We will climb together. And you will ask for my help." He brought his horse right next to hers, his knee bumping hers as he faced her.

"I won't." She poked at his chest. "Not from you."

"Do you care to make a wager on that?"

"Fifty bucks says I make it to the top without help," Ellen said.

"A poor wager. Hardly worth making." His heart began to pound in his chest as possibilities opened up before him.

"Well, excuse me, your high-and-mightiness. I don't carry bags full of gold fizz-cats—"

"Fiats." He corrected her.

"Whatever. I'm not a moneybags like you."

"Which is why a wager for money does not interest me." Rudi pretended to a nonchalance he did not feel.

"What does?"

"If," he said, crowding his mount deliberately into hers, making it back up a step, "if you ask for my help at any time while you are climbing the rock face, I win. If I win, you will agree to do whatever I ask for all of this night to come." He intended to require answers to all his questions.

"If you win, I'm your love slave?" Ellen's voice was colored with bitterness.

Her words made him burn, now she had spoken them, though his intentions truly did not go in this direction. "I suppose you could think of it that way. I did not."

"Sure you didn't."

"Believe what you will." He shrugged, as if it was of no matter to him.

"So I win if I get to the top on my own, right? What do I win? You as *my* love slave?"

"It sounds—" his attention was caught by the quick slide of her tongue across her lower lip "—sounds fair to me."

"It would. Either way, you get what you want."

Rudi backed his horse, as if preparing to leave. "If you are afraid…"

"Don't try to pull that on me. I know what you're trying to do. And you know I'm not afraid to climb that cliff." She stabbed a finger first at him, then toward the cliff.

"Yes. I know you are not afraid of rocks." Rudi crowded close again, urging his mount forward until he was eye-to-eye with Ellen. Understanding burst in his mind with all the slow-dawning power of a sunrise. "You are afraid of me. You are afraid of what I make you feel."

"Like hell I am." Ellen kicked her horse several times before it agreed to move. "You've got your bet."

He rode after her the few dozen yards to the base of the gray granite rock face. Though it was scarcely thirty feet high and studded generously with footholds and handholds, the cliff appeared twice as high and three times as dangerous, now that his mind visualized Ellen's slender form clinging to its side.

"Ellen, wait," he said, reining his horse in beside her as she dismounted.

"Second thoughts, Rudi?" She sent him a challenging glare. "Too late. Of course, if *you're* afraid…"

He was, but not for himself. "You could get hurt."

"I can get hurt walking through Central Park. I can get hurt going down the stairs in my building." She found handholds and set her foot on the first rock. "But I don't. I can take care of myself."

Rudi swung off his horse and hurried to her. "You cannot climb in those boots."

Ellen paused atop her rock and looked at her feet. "I hate to get my new boots all scuffed up. But too bad. You can polish them tonight when you're my slave." She shot him a wicked grin.

"No. That is not what I mean. The soles are too slick for climbing. They will slip." He held up his hands to assist her down.

"Those dozen times you climbed these rocks, did you wear cowboy boots?" She stood straight, balanced on the sizable boulder, waiting for his answer.

"Yes, but—"

"If you can do it, I can do it."

She started up again, checking each foothold before trusting her weight to it. At least she took proper caution, Rudi thought, following close behind her and just to her left. Even better, this rock face was not actually vertical. Not quite.

Hand by hand, foot by foot, they climbed the cliff. A dozen times, a score, a hundred, Rudi reached out to help Ellen, to lift her past a difficult spot, to catch her when her foot slipped yet again. And each time, Ellen glared his assistance away. His heart pounded like a runaway camel, his breath rasped in his ears, as if he climbed a sheer hundred-foot cliff, rather than this tiny one.

When they neared the top, Rudi scrambled ahead, ready to pull her up if necessary. Once more, Ellen refused his hand, crawling under her own power over onto the sparse grass growing in the gritty soil. Panting slightly, more from the altitude than the effort, he was sure, she grinned triumphantly at him as she got to her feet.

"I won," she said.

Rudi's control broke. He caught her by the shoulders and shook her. "Don't ever do that to me again!"

Then he wrapped his arms around her and held on tight, until his own shaking stopped, however long that might take. She was in his arms, whole and safe. He had not taunted her into killing herself.

"Hey, take it easy." Ellen pushed against him, but he could not let her go. Not yet.

"What's going on here?" Her voice came gentler this time. "Rudi?"

Still he could not release her, could not find words, though his heart finally began to slow.

"Rudi, were you worried about me?" This time Ellen managed to pry herself free, enough to look up into his face. "You didn't think I could do it, did you?"

He said nothing, but she must have seen the truth in his expression, for she tore herself free, stumbling back a few paces, knocking away his hands as he grabbed to keep her from the edge.

"How many times do I have to tell you?" Her eyes flashed blue lightning at him. "I can take care of myself."

"I know. That is—" He gave her a rueful look. "My head knows. But my heart is not so wise. It sees only the danger."

"Oh, please." Ellen rolled her eyes. "Let's leave any talk about hearts out of this. You don't mean it, and I don't need it."

Now Rudi's temper flared, but he kept a tight grip. "You do not know. Neither what I mean, nor what you need."

"And you *do?*" Her sarcasm inflamed him further.

"Yes." He bit the word out.

She answered with a snort of mocking laughter. Most unbecoming. "Just remember, princey." She put her forefinger against his chest and pushed. "I won. Tonight I own you. *Capiche?* I own *you.* Not the other way around."

"Yes." The words gritted between his teeth as he ground them. "I understand." He did not know *capiche,* but he could discern its meaning from the use she made of it.

He would be her slave tonight. Honor demanded it. And while he was her slave, he would do everything in his considerable power to break down the walls of fear behind which she hid.

Rudi glanced up at the sun beginning to descend toward the distant Sangre de Cristo Mountains. "We should go back now. Annabelle will have dinner waiting by the time we arrive.''

''I won.'' She taunted him in a childish singsong. ''Care to make another wager? Want to race down?''

''No!'' The shout burst from his sudden, stomach-clenching fear.

''Why not? Afraid you'll lose? Again?''

Her ridiculous glee would be amusing at another time, but not at the top of a thirty-foot cliff. Rudi caught her arm, hauling her close, letting her see his anger.

''Because the quickest way to the bottom is to fall,'' he hissed. ''I will go down first, and you will follow. And if I wish to help you, I will. And you will accept my help. Do you...*capiche?*''

She blinked, seemingly taken aback by his vehemence. ''Okay. Fine. You're the boss.'' A wicked little smile crept across her lips. ''Until tonight, that is.''

Rudi gave a single abrupt nod. ''Until tonight.''

Six

As they climbed back down the cliff face, Ellen was forced to admit that she was grateful for Rudi's help. Down turned out to be a lot harder than up. She lost count of the number of times he guided her foot to a better hold, or steadied her when the slick-soled boots threatened to slip. When they finally reached bottom, she had to hold on to Rudi's hands, the two hands that had steadied her those last steps from shaky rock to solid ground, for a few extra moments. Just long enough to make sure her knees would hold.

Halfway back to Rudi's house, reality hit her. She'd won the bet. She had won Rudi for her very own personal love slave for the night. What in the hell was she going to do with a love slave?

Okay, he'd tried to dress it up when he made the bet, just saying that the loser had to do whatever the winner demanded. But when she'd accused him of the love-slave thing, he hadn't denied it. He just hadn't expected to lose.

But he had. He'd lost, she'd won, and now she owned him for the night.

She could handle it. She was the boss. All she had to do was not ask for…that.

Ellen glanced at him, riding easily beside her. He looked good in a cowboy hat and jeans. Very natural. He'd looked just as good in his Arab clothes. *Face it, Ellen. He'd look good in anything.*

Or nothing.

She smashed that thought flat with a mental sledgehammer. Only, it curled up again, coming back to life like the villain in that silly Roger Rabbit movie. The man was temptation on the hoof, the devil with big brown eyes.

His shirt strained at the seams where it stretched across his shoulders, the snaps threatening to pop all on their own. She wanted to find out what was underneath. *No, she didn't.* His hips moved with the rhythm of the horse, his legs stretched wide around its barrel, and she wondered how those legs would feel… She tried again to deny the thought, and gave it up as useless. She did want, and wonder, and all the rest of it.

Sex with Rudi might be different, might be all those bells and whistles and fireworks going off that she'd heard about but never believed. With Davis, back when she still believed in true love and fairy-tale endings, sex had been okay, but nothing to write home about. She'd tried it a couple of times since then, thinking surely it had to get better, surely there had to be something to all those romance-novel descriptions. But it hadn't and there wasn't.

So she just wouldn't go there. She could think of plenty of things Rudi could do for her that didn't have anything to do with sex.

No, she couldn't.

When she looked at him, she wanted to touch him, and when she touched him, she wanted to— She just plain wanted.

She couldn't do this. She didn't need a love slave, didn't want a love slave. But she couldn't back out of it. That had been part of the dare. Rudi had accused her of being afraid of the prize. Of course, he was really saying that she was afraid to *be* the prize. Which was true, though she'd never tell him that.

Unfortunately, winning the prize seemed to be almost more frightening. If she tried to call it off, Rudi would accuse her of cowardice again, and she couldn't bear that. Maybe she was scared of certain things sometimes, but she couldn't let anyone know it.

Rudi had to be the one to back out. He was a sheikh. A prince. He was used to people bowing and scraping before him, not doing the scraping himself. Surely his pride wouldn't let him go through with this slave thing. Ellen sincerely hoped so.

If he didn't back out on his own, maybe she could help him along. Maybe she could be so demanding, so imperious, that he would get fed up and quit. She would have to try. Otherwise, disaster loomed.

* * *

When they arrived back at the house, Rudi took care of the horses, which Bill had trailered over earlier in the day. They belonged to Rudi, but usually they stayed in the barn near Bill's house, where he could care for them more easily. With a last pat of his mare's sleek gray rump, Rudi headed for the house and Ellen.

After a brief search, he found her on the deck outside the first-floor bedroom. Something jolted deep inside him at the sight of the sunlight on her golden hair, here in this place that he loved. The pines rising from the hillside beyond provided a fitting backdrop for her beauty.

"There you are." The expression on her face as she turned and spoke put Rudi on his guard. "What took you so long? I've been waiting for ages."

He might have been encouraged by her words if her face had not told him she plotted something. "The horses required care," he said. "I am here now."

"Did I say you could talk?" She drew herself up into a regal posture. "I don't care about your excuses. I don't care about the horses. I care about me. You're my slave, and you have to do what I say."

His eyes narrowed as he watched her watching him. If he were not certain she planned something devious, her latest words would make him angry. But somehow, he knew that anger was what she intended to provoke. Therefore he must remain calm until he perceived her purpose.

Rudi bowed in apology, remaining silent, as she demanded of him.

"Go get me something to drink," she ordered, waving her hand.

He waited.

"Well?" She raised her brows expectantly.

"What do you wish to drink?"

"I don't care. Something cold."

Rudi imitated Omar's bow again and turned to go.

"No, wait." Ellen called him back. "First, come take off my boots."

He inclined his head in acquiescence and approached her, holding his temper in firm hands. Bending over from the waist, he lifted her foot.

"No." She pushed him away. "You're not doing it right. I want you down. On your knees."

Rudi's eyes flashed to her, and he saw the look of triumph on her face before she hid it behind her mask. Immediately his anger cooled. She wanted him angry. She purposely tried to demean him in order to spark his temper. Why?

Slowly, holding her gaze, Rudi went down on one knee. She swallowed hard. He picked up her foot and tugged the boot off easily. He sent a caress of his thumbs across the arch of her foot, and Ellen gasped. With a hidden smile he set the foot down and picked up her other one. She was not immune to him.

As he removed this boot, still watching her, Rudi saw a flicker of apprehension cross her face, and he understood. She intended to push him until he backed out of the wager. Her pride would not allow her to back down, and she believed that his pride would not allow him to do her bidding.

She was wrong.

The Silhouette Reader Service™ — Here's how it works:

Accepting your 2 free books and gift places you under no obligation to buy anything. You may keep the books and gift and return the shipping statement marked "cancel." If you do not cancel, about a month later we'll send you 6 additional novels and bill you just $3.34 each in the U.S., or $3.74 each in Canada, plus 25¢ shipping and handling per book and applicable taxes if any.* That's the complete price and — compared to cover prices of $3.99 each in the U.S. and $4.50 each in Canada — it's quite a bargain! You may cancel at any time, but if you choose to continue, every month we'll send you 6 more books, which you may either purchase at the discount price or return to us and cancel your subscription.

*Terms and prices subject to change without notice. Sales tax applicable in N.Y. Canadian residents will be charged applicable provincial taxes and GST.

GET FREE BOOKS and a FREE GIFT WHEN YOU PLAY THE...

7 Lucky

Just scratch off the silver box with a coin. Then check below to see the gifts you get!

SLOT MACHINE GAME!

YES! I have scratched off the silver box. Please send me the 2 free Silhouette Desire® books and gift for which I qualify. I understand I am under no obligation to purchase any books, as explained on the back of this card.

326 SDL DFTV

225 SDL DFTU
(S-D-OS-11/01)

| | | | | | | | | | | | | | | | | | |

NAME

(PLEASE PRINT CLEARLY)

ADDRESS

APT.#

CITY

STATE/PROV.

ZIP/POSTAL CODE

7	7	7
🍒	🍒	🍒
♣	♣	♣
🔔	🔔	🍒

Worth TWO FREE BOOKS plus a BONUS Mystery Gift!

Worth TWO FREE BOOKS!

Worth ONE FREE BOOK!

TRY AGAIN!

Visit us online at www.eHarlequin.com

DETACH AND MAIL CARD TODAY!

He intended to make her feel every one of the things she was afraid of feeling, and he would do it by catering to each one of her whims. This would be a night Ellen Sheffield would never forget.

Somebody had sucked all the oxygen out of the atmosphere. Or maybe she'd just forgotten to breathe. Ellen tried inhaling, just as an experiment, but the air seemed to get caught in her throat somewhere before it actually made it to her lungs.

It was Rudi's fault, of course. His fault for having such big, deep, dark brown eyes, and looking at her with them. Looking at her like that. Not as if she was a trophy, or an expensive toy, or any of the other things men had told her in the past, but as if she was infinitely more valuable than anything in the world. As if she was cherished.

She jerked her foot out of his grip and shoved him with it. "Go on. Get me that drink."

Instead of glaring at her, or stomping away, or doing any of the things she expected, Rudi made that gracious, graceful bow of his head and rose smoothly to his feet. The muscles of his thighs bunched, making her bite her lip hard. The pain didn't distract her from the sight, from wanting to see just exactly how those muscles felt beneath her hands.

"Of course," he said. And he went to do as she ordered.

What was wrong with the man? Didn't he have any pride? If she had been the one to lose the bet, she'd be slamming doors and throwing things already.

Ellen sighed. Maybe it just meant he was a better

sport than she was. That didn't take much. She hated to lose. But somehow, some way, she had to make him back out of this bet. She couldn't take much more of those bedroom eyes or movie-star muscles.

He returned, carrying an opened bottle of beer on a tray, and bowed as he served it to her.

She glared at him as she snatched it up and took a drink, then she slammed it back on the tray. "I didn't want beer. I wanted a soda. Bring me something soft."

Still he didn't flare up. *Still,* he just bowed. "As you wish."

What did she have to do to make the man quit? She was beginning to feel bad about being so nasty to him. He was probably just as thirsty as she was. "Wait."

Rudi turned back, one eyebrow up as he waited for her next petty order.

"No use wasting the beer," she said. "You can have it if you want."

His smile was tiny, scarcely a smile at all, and it turned her insides into something soft and gooey, like chocolate pudding. She was in deep, deep trouble here.

"Thank you, *zahra.*"

Now he was using Arabic words on her. It probably meant "slave driver." He inclined his head in that minibow that she was rapidly getting sick of, and vanished back into the house.

Moments later he returned yet again, the beer on the tray now accompanied by a can of pop. Rudi served her, then set the tray on the bench beside her before collecting his bottle.

Ellen racked her brain, trying to think of something else she could do to stop this stupid situation. Her annoyance with him, with herself, and the whole situation, grew.

"Stop looming over me like that," she snapped. "I hate it when you loom."

Rudi grinned at her, and her heart took off on a race to nowhere. He sat back on his heels, hovering there with his knees near his armpits, and his backside inches off the decking. "First I am coy," he said. "And now I loom. What will you accuse me of next?"

"Did I say you could talk?" Ellen refused to look at that backside, taunting her as it hovered.

His little bow was almost mocking this time, hunkered down as he was. "Forgive me, *zahra*. I exist only to serve you."

"Oh, for—" Ellen sprang from her seat, almost knocking Rudi over. "Don't you have any pride? Any self-respect? How can you stand to grovel like this?"

He rose to face her in one smooth motion. "I do not grovel. I serve." His forehead crinkled, the way it did when he spoke of something serious. "It is a matter of honor. I lost the bet, therefore I must fulfill the wager. Honor is only satisfied by paying my debts willingly, cheerfully and thoroughly. Halfhearted, grudging service will not do."

Ellen's heart sank. With that kind of attitude, she would never get him to quit. She turned away and walked to the deck railing, staring out at the red sunset sky beyond the mountains. She didn't know what to do. She liked Rudi, she really did. But she didn't trust him.

All of her previous experience with men had taught her that they would do anything, say anything to get what they wanted. And what they all wanted was a notch on the bedpost. To be able to point to her and say, "See that beautiful woman over there? I did her."

Some of them wanted to own her, to turn her into a prize they could show off, the way Davis had. But none of them wanted any more than her surface—the face, the hair, the legs, the body. What was inside the package didn't matter to them. Which was why her appearance made such a terrific weapon in the business she'd chosen. They didn't expect to find anything beneath it, and it gave her the advantage of surprise.

Rudi might be different in a lot of ways, but not in that one. He still wanted to notch his post. Ellen didn't dare let down her guard. Liking him, wanting him, just made it that much harder.

She sighed and started to lower herself to the bench, when her thigh muscles screamed. Ellen confined herself to a gasp. She grabbed for the railing, managing to hold on to her soda while all the muscles in her body told her in no uncertain terms just how unhappy they were. Not only had she ridden a horse several miles, an activity using a complete set of muscles previously unknown to her, but she'd climbed an entire cliff. Up and back down again.

"Ellen? Are you all right?" Rudi's silky, sexy voice sounded in her ear.

"Ow." She couldn't manage more as she tried to straighten again. "No, I'm okay." She fended off his solicitude. She didn't need to like him any more than she already did, and she certainly didn't need him this close to her. "I just found a few muscles I didn't know I had."

"Can I help?"

"Aspirin." She nodded her head. "Aspirin sounds good."

Rudi's hands settled onto her shoulders and began to rub, his strong fingers finding the knotted soreness. "I am no expert, but I have picked up some techniques from various massage therapists in the past. Would you like…?"

"Aspirin," she repeated. She didn't dare let Rudi get anywhere near her with those magic hands. In fact, she would tell him to stop what he was doing, right now. Or maybe in just another minute.

"Are you sure?" His breath whispered warm across her ear, and Ellen shuddered.

She made herself duck away, a harder thing to do than flipping a sumo wrestler onto his back. She should know. She'd done both. "Just aspirin." Maybe if she said it enough times, she'd believe it.

"Didn't I smell some of Annabelle's famous cooking when I was inside?" Ellen said, trying to distract him. Or herself.

He bowed and swept a hand toward the house, playing the perfect servant again. So perfect, she wanted to smack him. Or kiss him.

His mouth drew her, mesmerized her, tormented her. It was his best feature, next to his eyes. And his shoulders. And his... Ellen stopped that line of thought. But she couldn't stop thoughts about his mouth, because somehow she couldn't make herself stop staring at it. It looked like such a kissable mouth. So why hadn't he kissed her with it?

Not that she wanted him to kiss her. She didn't. She didn't think she did, anyway. But she did wonder. Not one kiss. He hadn't even tried. Not even last night at her bedroom door. Kisses on the forehead didn't count. And it made her curious what a real kiss from that eminently kissable mouth would be like. Dangerously curious.

"Ellen?"

She heard Rudi speak from somewhere far distant, but she couldn't drag her demented mind from its focus.

"Ellen, why are you staring at—?" Rudi's mouth came closer. His breathing seemed ragged, but no more than her own.

She tried to focus. She really did. But the day's exertion must have tied her brain in as many knots as it had her muscles. She could neither think nor move.

"I must," he murmured.

And his mouth closed over hers.

The touch was light at first, a tentative caress that came again with more confidence. Ellen sighed, unable to summon even a moan, and let her body settle against Rudi. His hand cupped the back of her head as his mouth moved over hers. His arm around her back supported her, holding her in place.

At the touch of his tongue, Ellen opened to him, teased and tasted him. She took possession of his mouth, even as she surrendered her own to him. This was everything a kiss should be, and more. The kind of kiss she'd known had to be out there, but never believed could be found. Not by her. Not until now. Until Rudi.

She heard a groan, and thought it came from Rudi, though it might have been hers. His hand moved from the back of her head to her bottom, pulling her hips in tight. She could feel his arousal press hard against her stomach, and she pressed back.

At that moment her good sense recovered from its exhaustion and lifted its feeble head. What in the world was she doing?

Kissing Rudi, her body retorted. Her body wanted to keep on kissing, wanted to follow the tingle his mouth had started and see where it led. But her good sense already knew where this kiss would take her. Right into big-time trouble.

Besides sleeping with her client being unethical as hell, she knew herself well enough to know that her emotions would inevitably get tangled up in Rudi if she had sex with him. And inevitably, she would get hurt. There were too many obstacles between them.

He was a prince. His family had more money than God, or at least more money than Bill Gates, which was probably close to the same thing. She was just Ellen Sheffield, a nobody special who'd had the misfortune to be born with a pretty face.

She couldn't afford to fall even a little bit in love with Prince Rudi, however great the temptation. And

Ellen was firmly convinced that no one had ever been this tempted since that snake waved that apple under Eve's nose in the Garden of Eden.

Ellen pulled away, breaking the kiss gently. Already he was getting to her, making her reluctant to wound even his pride.

"Dinner?" she said. "Aspirin?"

He blinked, cleared his throat. "Yes," he said, releasing her. "Yes. Dinner."

Rudi stepped back, then turned and almost ran into the house. His swift departure might have hurt her feelings if she hadn't already decided this was best.

She followed at the fastest pace her aching body would allow. She'd expected her legs and her butt to hurt after sitting on that horse for so long, but her shoulders and back were killing her, too. Even the muscles running down her ribs below her arms hurt. Heck, even her ears hurt. She was still feeling them as she entered the kitchen.

Rudi closed the oven door and faced her, that disgustingly cute oven mitt still on his hand. "Is something wrong with your ears?"

"They hurt." She hobbled on into the kitchen area. "I didn't think I had any muscles in my ears."

Rudi chuckled. He shook off the mitt and came to inspect. "They are sunburned. You did not think to put sunscreen on them, did you?"

"I sunburned my ears? I have never in my life heard of sunburned ears." Ellen touched them gingerly. The pain was more of a burn than an ache, she realized.

"Did you never go to the seaside as a child?"

"Yes, but I never—" She paused, remembering. "I guess I did sunburn my ears, but the rest of me was so much worse, I didn't really notice." She poked him in the arm. "What happened to my aspirin, slave?"

"Yes, *zahra.*" He made that fancy hand flourish with his bow this time. "I live to serve you."

"I can do without the sarcasm."

"What sarcasm?" His expression was wide-eyed innocence. "Every word from my lips is sincere truth." Then he laughed at her disgusted look.

Rudi pulled out a chair from the kitchen table as he passed it. "Sit. I will get the aspirin and some ice in a glass for your drink. It must be warm by now."

"Thanks." Ellen couldn't hold back the groan as she shuffled to the chair. She was positive she heard her body creak when she lowered herself into it.

"I cannot bear to see you in such pain." Rudi opened the aspirin bottle, poured two into his hand and held them out to her.

Ellen took the bottle instead. "Give me that. Those, too." She picked the tablets carefully from his palm, not wanting to touch him more than necessary. She was avoiding temptation just now.

She shook another aspirin from the bottle and tossed all three into her mouth, washing them down with swig of warm pop. Nasty tasting. "This is a three-aspirin ache," she informed Rudi, setting the bottle down on the table with a thump.

"Please," Rudi said. "Dinner is not yet finished cooking. Please, allow me to give you a massage. It will help. I swear it."

Ellen believed him. His magic fingers had done

wonders for her shoulders. But she didn't dare. A massage would mean Rudi touching more than just her shoulders. He would touch her back and her neck and her legs. Probably even her bottom, considering it was one of the places that hurt the most.

At that thought, the leftover tingle from his kiss started up all over again. Between the tingling and the aching, she couldn't think. She could only want.

"I'm not taking off my clothes," she said. *Where did that come from?* She had intended to turn him down when she'd opened her mouth. At least, she thought she had.

"Your jeans are too heavy, and the blouse will be harsh against your skin." His thumbs dug into the knots on either side of her spine and she moaned with the pleasure-pain of it.

When had he gotten close enough to do that to her again? He was right, though. The gingham collar felt rough as he rubbed her neck. Rudi moved it aside and laid his hand on bare skin, easing her aches. It did feel much better that way.

"It is, of course, your decision," he said, his voice low and seductive. "I am merely your servant, and do only as you bid. You may feel safe with me."

Safe? Not hardly. But it wasn't Rudi's action that endangered, it was her own reaction to him. Odd as it might seem, given her past experience, she trusted him utterly to go only as far as she invited. She just didn't know if she could keep from issuing a blanket invitation. Something along the lines of *Here I am. Take me.*

"Ellen?" Rudi lifted her to her feet. It wasn't as

painful a process when her own muscles did so much less of the work. He led her to the bedroom door.

"Lie down on the bed," he said. "Leave whatever clothing you feel appropriate, and call me when you are ready."

She went into the room and stared at the massive four-poster bed with its white textured coverlet. This was too hard. If she did as Rudi suggested, as her body demanded, she had sole responsibility for whatever happened. She couldn't blame Rudi for anything other than being himself. Could she handle a massage, or would it make her want more? And if she did want more, was she too afraid of being disappointed or hurt to risk it? Was that what had her dithering in the middle of the room?

"Coward." She hissed the word out loud.

Just because she accepted a massage didn't mean anything else *would* happen. Only that it *could.* She was the one in control tonight. Rudi had said that it was a matter of honor for him to obey her commands. To fulfill her wishes. He would stop if she asked him to. She knew it bone deep, as more than fact.

Ellen grabbed her shirt collar and yanked, popping the snaps open all the way down. She would take one step at a time. She would see how things went, and if she wanted to take the next step... Well then, she would. But she left her bra and panties on anyway as she crawled painfully onto the bed.

"I'm ready."

Rudi started at the sound of Ellen's voice calling from the bedroom. She was ready. But was he?

He took a deep breath, then shook himself, like a sprinter trying to loosen up before a race. Rudi didn't need to get loose, however. He needed tight, iron-hard control. He took another deep breath, closing his hands into fists.

"Rudi?"

"I am coming." He let the air out of his lungs as he reminded himself one more time that Ellen expected him to rebel against her instructions, and that therefore he must obey them perfectly. And he walked into the room.

The sight of her lying facedown on his bed, wearing only wispy scraps of pale blue silk, had him breathing deeply again, this time in hopes of holding his head in place on his shoulders. It threatened to fly away like a balloon. She was more beautiful than even his fertile imagination had pictured. Perhaps because this vision was real.

He put his knee on the bed and Ellen looked up, alarm in her eyes. "The bed is too wide," he said. "I cannot reach you properly unless I am on it with you."

"Oh." She nodded, accepting his excuse. "Okay."

She turned her face into the pillows again, her forehead resting on her folded hands.

Rudi clenched his hands tight once more before relaxing them and setting them on the smooth, silken skin of her shoulders. Then he dug his thumbs in, searching for the corded knots.

Ellen moaned. The sound twisted its way inside him to settle hot and heavy at his groin. This was going to be sheer torture.

He worked on her shoulders, slipping her bra straps out of the way. Then he moved down her back to the muscles between her shoulder blades. Ellen's moans and gasps sang counterpoint to the motion of his hands, arousing him as much as did touching her, for he imagined much the same music as he made love to her.

He massaged her deltoids, muscles he knew would be sore from the climb, and on down her sides.

"May I unfasten this?" He tugged lightly at the hooks fastening her bra, asking permission when he wanted to do as he wished.

"Go ahead," Ellen mumbled past her hands, giving him the freedom he desired.

Rudi had no oils for this massage and regretted his sparsely equipped toiletries. He had never brought a woman—or anyone, for that matter—to his New Mexico hideaway, and had seen no need for more than the basics. He would simply have to make do.

His hands rubbed their way down her back, using Ellen's "music" as a guide to the places that needed his attention.

"Better?" he asked.

"Mmm." She took a deep breath, her back rising with it. "Much."

He let his palms slide lightly over her soft skin, delighting in the feel, in the knowledge that she allowed him this freedom. "Where else? Your arms? Your legs?"

She straightened one of her arms, lifting it slightly. "It might do me some good."

Rudi massaged both arms, one after the other. Then he worked on the leg she raised into the air, rubbing her calves.

"Keep going," she said, when he would have stopped at her knees. She turned her head so the bedding didn't muffle her words. "The hurt goes all the way up. The cure needs to follow it."

"As you wish, *zahra.*" *Zahra.* Flower. A perfect description of Ellen, so delicate, so beautiful and fragrant. He would not survive this sweet torture. Touching her like this without promise of release was worse than any torments devised by his ancestors. Scorpions would be more welcome.

The sounds she made as he massaged her thighs intensified his arousal and thus his pain. He knew he should have changed out of jeans into native dress before beginning this. But if he had, his condition would be so obvious, he would doubtless frighten her back behind her mental walls.

"Anything else?" he asked, sitting back on his heels, sincerely hoping he would be given the chance to escape.

Ellen lifted her hips slightly and tightened her shapely buttocks. Rudi's mouth went dry. The tiny scrap of pale blue cloth covering them did not hide anything from his eyes. Any effect on modesty was purely imaginary.

"My bottom is sore, too. From the horse, I guess," she said in a faint, almost girlish voice. "Would you...?"

"At your command."

Seven

Ellen was on fire. Her whole, entire body burned, head to toe, front to back, inside and out. Every blood cell in every capillary in every tiny inch of Ellen blazed merrily away, and every bit of it was Rudi's fault.

The man was seduction made flesh, and now Mr. Temptation Personified had his hands on her bottom.

Why had she bothered to leave her panties on? They made no difference whatsoever. She could feel the warm texture of his palms right through the thin fabric. As he massaged the soreness away, which surely had not been so bad, the flames skittered around inside her. They collected in her secret places, where they burned higher, wilder.

"May I—?" Rudi's voice went rough and ragged, breaking off before he finished.

"What?" She sounded as ragged as he. If they had that in common, did they have the fires in common, too?

He answered without words, his fingers sliding beneath the elastic of her panties to set off new conflagrations everywhere he touched. Ellen lifted her hips, her good sense utterly burned away. Consequences be damned. She wanted this.

Rudi whisked the useless garment away and cupped her bottom in both his hands. Over the pounding of her heart, Ellen could hear the rasp of Rudi's breath, and she willed his hands to move, to touch her more, to give her the magic she knew they possessed.

He cleared his throat. "What is it you wish of me, my owner? To drive me mad? I have sworn to please you, but I am only a man, made of flesh and blood. I am not a stone."

His hands trembled where they touched her, and yet they did not move, other than a gentle squeeze, as if he still attempted his massage. Rudi spoke of desire, yet he did not act on it. Ellen knew he waited for her decision.

"What do you want me to do?" He sounded almost desperate.

She lifted her head and looked at him over her shoulder. His eyes blazed with dark fire as they locked on hers. No wonder she burned. But she couldn't accuse him of arson, not when she'd been dry fuel to his flame, ready to go up at the first touch.

"Please me," she said, turning on her side and

reaching out with one hand. "Make me feel good. Make love to me."

Rudi took her hand and let her draw him alongside, a smile curving his beautiful lips. "That is a terrifying command to give a man. What if I fail? What if I can merely make you feel 'not so bad'?"

Ellen popped the snaps on the shirt he still wore, feeling underdressed, and set her hand on his sleek, bare chest. "Then you'll just have to try again, won't you?"

He laughed. He caught her hand and pressed a kiss to her palm, the tingle acting like gasoline on those flames. He put her hand back on his chest, wriggled out of his shirt and sent it flying. He picked up her bra where it lay half on Ellen and half on the bed and sent it after his shirt. Then he stopped.

Rudi looked at her, his gaze flashing from her head to her toes and back. Then he urged her over onto her back, and he looked again, slowly. His fingers brushed where he looked, light as a breeze whispering over her skin.

Ellen had been ogled before. She had been looked at with greedy eyes, hungry eyes, envious eyes. Sometimes—once or twice—she had even been naked. She had never had any man look at her like this, as if she was a gift from God, something infinitely precious, to be admired and cherished. There was that word again. Cherished. It was ridiculous, but that was the way Rudi made her feel.

As his hand still swept featherlight over her shoulders, past the side of her breast, over her stomach, touching her everywhere but where she most wanted it, Rudi bent over her. He kissed her lips, a sweet, gentle touch. But Ellen was way past gentle.

Clasping his head between her hands so he couldn't escape, she opened her mouth and invited him to plunder with a quick, hard sweep of her tongue. Rudi didn't need a second invitation. He rolled half on top of her, his shoulders pressing her into the bed as his tongue plunged deep into her mouth and his hand burrowed to cup her bottom. He thrust a jeans-clad leg between hers and pulled her in tight.

He didn't leave much room for Ellen to go hunting for a zipper, but she found it. She had it halfway down before he caught her hand, stopping her.

"Wait." He panted, his forehead resting on hers, his eyes squeezed tight shut. "Do not do that."

Ellen tipped her face up and kissed the end of his nose. "Aren't you forgetting something, slave boy?" she teased.

Rudi groaned. He took two deep breaths and eased her hand away before attempting to speak. "You asked me to make you feel good. And I will, but—I said before, I am only a man. You make me so mad with desire—" He broke off to breathe again.

His words made Ellen a little crazy, too. He wanted her, worse than anyone she'd ever seen. But he was fighting like a demon against his own desires in order to give her what she wanted.

"Please," he said. "If you touch me there, I cannot do as you bid me do. Help me in this one thing."

"Oh, Rudi." Tears gathered in the corners of her eyes.

She'd never heard anything so wonderful, that this

strong, proud man would ask for her help at this moment. She cupped his face in her hands, the sandpaper roughness sweet against her palms, and she looked at him. She looked so deep into his dark eyes, she thought she could see his soul looking back at her. Ellen kissed him.

The minute their lips touched, the flames leapt up again, higher than before, consuming her as they burned. Rudi's hand lay flat against her stomach, warm and heavy. Slowly, so slowly she wanted to scream, his hand moved lower. Her hips rose, acting almost on their own, wanting him to hurry. But he refused.

He kissed his way down her neck, leaving a moist, chill snail trail of Rudi-kisses where he passed. He circled her breasts with those kisses, teasing her with them, the way he teased her below, combing his fingers through her crisp hair.

When she thought she would either scream or pass out, Rudi's mouth closed over the peak of one breast at the same moment his fingers found her hidden nub, and she did scream. Ellen came up off the bed with the explosion. The shocks went through her for eternal minutes as Rudi held her tight, whispering Arabic nothings she hoped were as sweet as they sounded.

Though more than she'd ever known in her life, it still wasn't enough, wasn't all she knew Rudi could give her. She pushed him back, grabbing the waist of his jeans and peeling them off as he hurriedly lowered the zipper the rest of the way. When he was naked, she paused to look at him where he stood beside the bed, glorying in the way he fit together, like that statue of David she'd seen in pictures. Thank goodness he was flesh and blood, rather than stone. Marble was pretty, but not near as much fun.

Ellen opened her arms. "Come here, you."

Rudi smiled and made his traditional obeisance. "At your command, *zahra*."

He paused to retrieve protection, and fit himself into the space she'd made for him, in the circle of her arms and legs, his belly burning against her heat.

He kissed her, deep and passion filled, but this kiss was tender at the same time, and heart-stoppingly sweet. When he ended the kiss, Rudi lifted his head and looked at her, cradling her face between his long-fingered hands. "Are you sure?" he asked.

Such a stupid question didn't deserve an answer. Ellen reached between their bodies, Rudi rising onto his knees to allow her access, and she guided him to her entrance. She locked her ankles behind his back, but before she could tighten them, he surged into her with one powerful thrust.

She was lost, and only Rudi could find her. She was blind, and deaf, oblivious to everything but the man in her arms and the sensations he created as he drove into her. Ellen met each stroke eagerly, feeling the flames leap higher with each one. His muscles bunched and moved under her hands, taut with the effort of his passion. Her cries echoed his, until with a shout, her world came apart again. She heard Rudi's shout a fraction of a second later, felt his body throb and shudder as he reached the same pinnacle. Ellen drifted back to earth, nothing more than white flakes of ash in the breeze.

* * *

He must have dozed. Or perhaps his spirit had simply left his body. Rudi was not certain which, though when he regained his senses, he discovered that he had at least moved to one side so that his weight did not crush Ellen.

Several minutes more passed before he realized what had roused him. A smell, sharp and acrid.

"Smoke!" He scrambled from the bed and rushed into the kitchen to discover the thing he smelled wisping from the edges of the oven. When he opened the door, smoke boiled out, setting the alarm to shrieking.

Ellen appeared in the bedroom doorway, naked, her gun in her hand. "Get down," she ordered.

"It is our dinner." Rudi fanned the smoke away. "Not terrorists." He put on the protective glove and pulled the burned food from the oven as Ellen came to join him.

"Where's the alarm?" she asked.

Rudi pointed to the thing directly overhead, though she surely could have found it by the sound alone. As he set the pan of food on the counter and closed the oven, Ellen pulled a chair over, climbed up on it and pressed the button, switching off the alarm. Then they looked at each other.

Ellen laughed first. "You know, the first time I saw you wearing that oven mitt, I thought you looked awfully cute. But this look is much, much better."

Only then did Rudi realize that the glove was the only garment he wore. He blessed their dinner for burning, for easing that first awkward afterward. He put his gloved arm around her, lifting her off the chair and sliding her down his body to the floor.

''Your attire is also very becoming.'' He held up her hand with the pistol. ''Is this the latest Paris accessory for such occasions?''

She stuck her tongue out at him. Then her face went solemn. ''For bodyguards who are so unethical as to get themselves into these occasions, I guess it is.''

Rudi sensed her withdrawal and kissed her, trying to put all he felt into the kiss. When she melted against him, he dared to break away for a moment. ''Does my owner have any other commands for me? Did I please her?''

Her sly smile made him want to crow in triumph. ''It's possible,'' she said. ''But I think we ought to try again, just to be sure.''

He began to protest that even a slave needed rest, when he realized that he did not. Ellen proved to be more powerful than any of the concoctions he had heard whispered about among the men at home. Rudi lifted Ellen in his arms and bore her into the bedroom. He paused to deposit the oven mitt and the pistol on the bedside table, then set about fulfilling the instructions of his temporary owner.

Ellen's first thought when she woke up the next morning was that she had been through a beating and left to die. Then she remembered. The horse, the cliff and Rudi.

He still lay in the bed beside her, facedown, smashed into the pillows, arms and legs sprawled as if laying claim to the entire mattress. Just like a man.

She smiled and resisted the temptation to twine one of his sable curls around her finger. She had things to do first. Things she would get to just as soon as a hot shower steamed some of the ache away. Of course, without Rudi's massage, Ellen didn't think she would have been able to move at all. Carefully she slid out of bed and hobbled into the bathroom.

The shower made her body feel almost human again, and the coffee finished the job. Her outsides began to match her insides, which felt superhuman. She couldn't stop smiling, thinking of last night. Rudi was more than she'd ever dreamed possible. His tender seduction had made her believe again. Surely he could never have showed such care for her pleasure if she meant nothing more than a conquest.

She took a quick gulp of the coffee, scalding her tongue, and picked up the phone on the kitchen wall. It might be a little late, but if she resigned now, maybe the fallout wouldn't be too bad.

"Hey, Jan, it's me," she said when the phone was answered in New York.

"Ellen?" The receptionist's voice dropped to a near whisper. "Where have you been? Mr. Campanello's about to start frothing at the mouth."

She frowned. "He knows where I am. Oh, never mind, Jan, just put me through. I'll see if I can calm him down."

"Sheffield!"

Ellen moved the phone away from her ear, but kept it close to her mouth. "Hey, boss."

"Where the hell are you? You're fired, you hear me?" The bellow suddenly ceased and became a near whimper, allowing her to move the earpiece closer.

"How could you do this to me? Those Arab clients have been giving me all kinds of grief, because that prince vanished again. I need you, Sheffield."

"But…" Ellen was confused. "I told Marco I was with Rudi. Rudi said—"

"Who the hell is Rudi?" Campanello was back to bellowing.

Understanding dawned. Rudi wasn't his name. It was just a nickname. She'd thought of him as Rudi for so long that it hadn't occurred to her that she was probably the only person in the world who did.

"Rudi is Rashid. Prince Rashid." She sank into a kitchen chair, hand over her eyes to hide her pain from the squirrels outside the window.

"You're with the prince? That's great! Where are you? Why didn't you report in?"

"I just did. Rudi—that is, Rashid—told me this trip was cleared." Of course it hadn't been. She realized that now.

He had skipped town without telling anyone and had made her an accessory to his flight. He'd taken a risk letting her call in to check, but it had paid off for him. Big time.

"I thought you knew where we were."

"And where is that?"

"New Mexico. A place Ru—Rashid has near the mountains. It's a great safe house." Ellen wiped away the tears, tasting the bitter salt of her own stupidity.

"Good. Looks like we're going to need it. The cops have spotted one of those Qarif terrorists in New York. Here's what I want you to do."

"Wait. I thought I was fired."

"Get outta here. You're not fired. You're a vice president, for cryin' out loud. You're my partner."

"Well, then, I quit."

"You can't quit, either. Partners don't quit on each other. I need you on this one. How long we been together, Sheffield?"

"I don't know. Six years."

"Six years. Practically since you finished the academy and came on the job. Remember? Who was there when you dumped that rat Lowe?"

"You." Oh Lord, was he going to go through the whole litany again?

"Who was there when those jerks in the precinct went after you 'cause you got promoted so fast?"

"You, boss, okay? You don't have to—"

"Who was there when—"

"I got the message, okay?" She broke in on his recital. "It's just—I can't work this job anymore, boss." She tried hard to keep the tears out of her voice, but she didn't succeed. "It wouldn't be ethical."

Silence stretched as Campanello absorbed the meaning behind her words. "Oh, geez, Sheffield. Why'd you have to go and fall in love with the guy?"

"I'm not in love with him." She couldn't be. She was just another notch on the bedpost to him.

"If you slept with him, you're in love with him. I know you. We been through this before. Geez, Sheffield, what happened to my Ice Princess, huh?"

"I don't know." The tears fell harder, let loose by Campanello's rough sympathy. "I lost my mind, I guess."

"Okay, here's what I need you to do—"

"Vic, didn't you hear me? I have to resign from this job."

"Do this first. Then I'll let you quit. You're the only guy I got on the spot, Ellen. I really do need you."

She sighed, swiping uselessly at her eyes. "Okay, boss. But you owe me."

"I always owe you something, Sheffield. What's new?" He paused. "Are you gonna be okay with this?"

Ellen took a deep breath. If Vic Campanello was acting this nice to her, she must really sound in bad shape. "Yeah. I'll make it." She had to.

"Okay, so now can I tell you what I want you to do?"

Her chuckle was feeble, but it was there. Her boss was one of the good guys. "Go ahead."

"We can use this safe house for big brother Ibrahim's family. They think some of those terrorists got out of Qarif, and they think they're probably coming over here. So what I need you to do is this."

As she listened to her instructions, Ellen built back her weak defenses, ready to topple over at the next perfect smile from that snake. To fortify them, she enumerated Rudi's faults. He was arrogant. He was a smart-ass. He had lied to her.

This whole trip had been one big lie. Except for the thing with the well in town. And he'd used that one bit of truth to build all his lies on.

He'd lied when he told her his family knew about the trip. He'd lied when he said her boss knew about it. But the worst, biggest lie was when he had made her believe he cared about her.

He didn't cherish her any more than a lion cherished the zebra it ate. He fussed about her climbing the cliff only because if she fell and killed herself, he wouldn't get his notch. But she had been the one stupid enough to believe every soulful look. And she was still dumb enough to wish they'd been true.

"Stupid," Ellen hissed aloud as she gathered up what little gear she had. "Stupid, stupid, stupid."

She took the clothes. She would need them. But she left the cowboy boots standing beside the bedroom door.

Rudi woke slowly after his night of slavery. He lay cocooned in the sheets for an age, remembering every delicious moment of the experience, before he stretched out an arm, seeking Ellen. The other side of the bed was cool, its occupant long gone.

Slitting an eye open, he saw the sun spots on the floor near the windows, indicating a time shortly past noon. After the night's exertions, he had needed to recoup his energies. The night was over. Now it was time for the day's delights. A shower would make a good beginning. If Ellen would not scrub his back, surely he could convince her to let him scrub hers.

He wrapped the sheet around him in a sort of djellaba and went to find her. "Ellen?"

As he stepped through the bedroom entrance, the door to his house burst open and a riot spilled through it. A riot made up of Ibrahim's four children, their mother, Kalila and, herding them all before him, his brother Ibrahim.

Eight

"**R**ashid, are you ready to go to work?" Ibrahim paused near the hotel-suite door and looked back at Rudi.

With a sigh, Rudi rose from the sofa where he'd been sitting, elbows propped on his knees, and threw the folds of his kaffiyeh back from his face. "I *was* working. You took me away from it."

"*Tchah!* You were playing with the woman."

"I. Was. Working." Rudi made each word a complete sentence, knowing even so that his brother would pay no attention.

"Digging holes in the ground is not the work of a prince of Qarif." Ibrahim opened the door and waited for Rudi to go through. "You are a child playing with mud pies. Rashid, you are twenty-eight years old. It is time you stopped playing in the dirt and did the work of a man.''

''Digging holes in the ground brought you all of that money you love so much,'' Rudi said, his anger ready to explode.

''We hired other people to do it. We pay them to get their hands dirty.''

''Because none of us know how to do it. Now we know. I know. And I am very good at it.''

''You?'' Ibrahim's face showed the same affectionate contempt as always. He laughed, cuffing Rudi on the shoulder as he shoved him into the elevator.

The bodyguards followed. Rudi was certain he felt the elevator groan from the weight of muscle and weapons.

''You are good at causing your father's gray hairs and your mother's tears,'' Ibrahim said, almost sadly. ''And at causing a great deal of trouble for me. We should never have allowed you to go to that ridiculous university in Texas. What was it? Texas Engineering—''

''Texas Tech University,'' Rudi corrected automatically. On the west Texas plains, it had reminded him a little of Qarif's open spaces. Those had been the happiest years of his adult life, because he had been free to study whatever interested him and to make friends of whomever he chose. Those friends had given him his nickname, calling him Rudolph Valentino when they learned his father was a sheikh. It had quickly been shortened to Rudi. He preferred the nickname, because he knew that those who used it saw the man that he was, rather than the man they wished him to be.

As they got into the car, Ibrahim began talking numbers. Rudi understood numbers, but he understood them when related to things like pressure, or the tensile strength of a certain thickness of steel. He had no interest in high finance or manipulating money that existed only in theory. Money was to spend in building things. Or in buying gifts for beautiful women.

Why had Ellen left the boots? In the uproar surrounding the installation of Ibrahim's family in the ranch house, and the flight back to New York, Rudi had had no time to think about what it might mean. But now he had more than enough time.

The instant Rudi had seen his brother's family invading what had been his private sanctuary, the one place where he could have peace from his family's demands, he had known that Ellen had discovered his prevarications. *Call it by its true name. You lied to her.* Ibrahim's presence was her return volley in this game they had played.

He understood Ellen's anger upon discovering that neither his family nor her employer had known where they had gone. Her move had been quite clever. Diabolical. His secret hideaway was secret no longer. When he had learned the reasons behind the children and Kalila coming to the ranch, he had no more objections. They would indeed be far safer in the mountains.

So why had she left the boots? Surely she did not think he had offered them as payment for the gift of her body. Had he not shown her how he treasured her? Did not his care for her pleasure before his own tell her how very precious she was to him?

The surprised delight on her face as he introduced her to the wonders of her senses should have told him of her inexperience, but he had been so overwhelmed himself. He found it difficult to believe of a woman in her culture with her beauty, but now, thinking back, he knew it was so.

What if that inexperience had led her to believe that the whole of his intent in bringing her to his home had been seduction? Could she think he cared nothing more for her than that, think he had no more use for her, now he had made love to her? Did she think everything that had happened was merely part of the game?

It was time for the game to end. Everything had suddenly become all too real.

"Stop the car." Rudi reached forward and rapped on the glass separating them from the driver.

"Don't be ridiculous," Ibrahim said as the glass descended and the car slowed. "Drive on."

"I said, stop the car," Rudi repeated. He reached for the door and opened it while the car was still moving.

"Stop the car!" Ibrahim grabbed for him, but Rudi was already out of the car and striding down the street.

When he looked back, Rudi saw Frank and Omar trotting after him. He sighed, then slowed to wait for them.

"Have you come to take me back?"

"No." Frank was panting. "Just stay with you, is all he said."

"Good." Rudi turned, his robes swirling about him, and walked on.

Ellen stared at the paperwork on her desk, trying to make sense of what she saw, but it was no good. She'd left her mind at home in bed. Or maybe she'd left it in New Mexico. On second thought, that had to be the answer. Because while in New Mexico, she had certainly lost her mind.

She could think of no other reason for doing the things she'd done. She had simply lost her mind. And when it had gone missing, her body had needed very little convincing to believe that Rudi was different, when he was just the same as all the other men in the world.

The intercom buzzed at the same time her office door flew open. Rudi strode through it, looking like something out of *Lawrence of Arabia,* with Jan the receptionist and two bodyguards on his heels. Dear Lord, she was not ready for this.

"I'm sorry—" Jan said.

"Leave us." Rudi cut her off, his peremptory tone and the brusque wave of his hand setting Ellen's teeth on edge.

She'd known all along this was the man he was. Why did it bother her now?

Omar backed out of the room, but Frank and Jan hovered.

"Ellen?" Jan said. "I couldn't stop him. I tried..."

Rudi turned and glared, but they held their ground,

waiting for Ellen's decision. She took a deep breath. She didn't want this confrontation, but one thing she had learned about Rudi: The man was as stubborn as a rock. If she didn't talk to him now, he'd probably kidnap her again.

"It's all right," she said. "I'll talk to him."

The minute the door closed, leaving the entourage on the far side, Rudi's expression changed. Gone was the imperious autocrat, and in its place Ellen saw the tender lover of her nightmares.

"Why did you leave so precipitously?" He crossed the room toward her.

Ellen held her position, telling herself that she was not using her desk as a barricade to hide behind. Good thing, because it made a lousy barricade. Rudi walked around it and dropped to one knee beside her chair.

"We could have traveled together," he said.

Ellen shrugged, trying to shrug off the pain with an air of unconcern. "I thought it was better that way. I figured you'd had all the togetherness you wanted."

The puzzled crease between his eyebrows made her want to touch it, to caress it away. She made her hands into fists and pushed her chair back, hoping it would help her resist the impulse.

"How can you say that, *zahra?*" he said. "You know—"

"Stop calling me that!" She cut off his speech, springing out of the chair in her agitation. "I don't own you, okay? I never did."

Rudi frowned up at her, still down on one knee. "What do you think *zahra* means?"

"I don't know." Ellen glanced at Rudi as he rose

to his feet. Maybe if he turned that headdress around so it covered his face she might be able to think straight.

"No, you do not. But what do you *believe* that it means?"

"Owner. Mistress. Slave driver. Simon Legree." She threw her hands up and retreated to the opposite side of her small office. "I have no idea."

"*Zahra* means flower." He came around to the front of the desk, following her.

"I'm not a stupid flower. I don't wilt in the sun." She moved toward the slice of window she shared with the office next door and stared out at the pigeons. "Stop following me."

"Stop running away." Rudi halted in the middle of the room. "The flowers in Qarif do not wilt in the sun, either. They turn their faces to it, welcoming the light. They bloom from strength, with deep roots and proud branches."

Ellen took a deep breath, trying to steel herself against his seductive lies. He had charm by the bucketful, but that's all it was, charm that evaporated when you looked closely.

"Look, Rudi." She turned back to face him and forgot what she was going to say. Why did he have to look at her like that?

"Yes, Ellen?" he prompted.

She took a deep breath and huffed it out. This was going to be hard. "Look. Either tell me why you came here this morning, or let me get back to work."

"I came to see you. To learn why—" He broke off and looked down at his feet. "Actually, I do understand that you were angry because I allowed you to believe the trip had been cleared by your employer. I came..." He looked up at her then, his eyes locked onto hers. "I came to ask your forgiveness."

Ellen blinked. *Damn him.* She could not let him do this to her again. "Okay. You're forgiven. Anything else?" She stepped toward her desk and picked up a piece of paper, hoping she was holding it right side up, because she couldn't read a thing on it.

"No, that is not all." He plucked the paper from her fingers and laid it on her desk. "Have dinner with me tonight. Have lunch with me now. Have breakfast with me tomorrow morning."

Pain dug spiky fingers into her heart. Why did it still hurt her? "No," she said.

Rudi's hand froze in midair, stopped as he reached for her hand. "No?"

"You heard me the first time." She eased another step away from him.

"But...why?"

Ellen busied herself, straightening papers into semineat stacks. "We had a great time in New Mexico, Rudi. But it's over. We're back in New York, and it's time to move on."

"I do not wish to move on." He caught her arm and turned her toward him. "It is not over. I want to be with you, Ellen. When I am alone, I am half a man. I did not know it until I met you."

She laughed, forcing the sound past the threatening tears. "Do they teach 'How To Use Words for Seduction' in school where you come from? That's a real pretty speech. How many times have you used it?''

"Never. Not before this moment. It is true. It is how I feel. Marry me, Ellen. I cannot bear to be without you.''

Shock raced through her, staggered her. Ellen braced a hand against her desk. When she looked at Rudi, she saw the same stunned expression she knew had to be on her own face. He had not expected the words, either.

"You don't mean that,'' she said.

"I do. Marry me.'' He said it again. He caught her hand before she could pull it back and held on tight, carrying it to his lips, where he pressed a kiss to the back. "Marry me.''

Gathering all her strength, both physical and emotional, she yanked her hand from his grasp. "Rudi, be reasonable. We both know you don't want to marry me.''

"Stop saying that. You do not know what I want.''

"Do you?''

"Who better? Of course I know.''

Ellen circled to the front of her desk again, seeking room to pace. "I don't think so. You don't have a clue who I am. How long have we known each other, when you add it all up? Three days?''

"It seems I have always known you.''

"I'm not sure it's even three days. Rudi, you just want what you see.'' She waved her hand along her body. "But this isn't me.''

"It is you,'' he said. "But only a tiny part.''

"It's not me at all. But it's all you see. I won't be your trophy, Rudi. I am not some rich man's toy."

"Is that what you think I want?" Rudi snatched off his headdress and shook it in her face, the gold cords rattling faintly. "This is all that you see when you look at me, is it not? Do not accuse me of your own faults."

He threw the cloth across the room, then ripped off the robe he wore and sent it sailing after the headdress, standing before her wearing an open-necked white dress shirt and gray slacks. "I am only a man who has done nothing more than ask a woman to marry him."

Taken aback by all the flying fabric, Ellen had to pause to marshal her thoughts. "Why?" she said.

Rudi frowned. "What?"

"It's a simple question. Just one word. You want a couple more words? Fine. Why do you want to marry me? And don't say because you love me, because I won't believe it. People don't fall in love overnight. They fall in lust. That's all this is."

"It is not." He spaced the words out, his hands clenching again and again, as if he fought violent passions.

"I think it is. We had us one fine case of lust."

"You are wrong, Ellen. What we had was far more than mere lust."

Why did he have to keep insisting? "Well, I think I'm right." She rubbed her temples, a headache beginning to throb behind her eyes. She had to end this, get her life back.

"Look, Rudi, I'm not going to marry you." She

retreated behind her desk. "I suggest that you sit down and think real hard about your life. You decide what it is you really want, and why you want it."

She paused, but she couldn't stop there. Maybe she was the world's biggest idiot for wanting to believe that at least some of what Rudi said might possibly be true, but she couldn't help it.

"And when you get it all straight in your head," she said, somehow forcing the tears back, "if you still have a place for me in that life you decide you want, come back and see me, and tell me why you want me there. And maybe I'll have a different answer."

Rudi took a deep breath. He rubbed a hand over his mouth before looking up at her. "You will not marry me." It wasn't a question.

"No." She just couldn't take the risk. Not now.

He walked across the room and stared at his robes. "Who was the man who hurt you so badly? The man who wanted to own you for his plaything?"

Cold chills shivered down her back. Who had told him? "What makes you think there was a man?"

"Tell me his name, Ellen." Fire flashed from his eyes as he glared at her.

"Davis Lowe. Wh-why? Why do you want to know?"

"So I can know it, while I decide whether I will kill him."

He hesitated a moment, then crossed the room in two steps and caught her by both arms. Before she could even gasp, he kissed her, not with fierce passion as she might have expected, but deep, slow, wet, and so tender she could have wept with his sweetness.

When he ended the kiss she had not made up her mind whether to push him away or pull him closer.

"And that," he said, "is so that you will know what it is you have discarded." With that, he threw his robes over his arm and strode from her office. Frank and Omar trotted after him.

When the coast was clear, Jan scurried back and peeped through the still-open door to Ellen's office. "Are you okay? What did he want?"

Would Rudi really kill Davis? Maybe she ought to call and warn him. Or maybe not. If any man deserved killing...

Oh, good grief. Davis hadn't done anything worth killing him over, nothing any other man didn't do every day of his life. Of course Rudi wasn't going to kill Davis.

"Ellen?" Jan rapped her knuckles on the door.

"Hmm?" Ellen shook her head, trying to unscramble her brain.

"So what did he want? The cute sheikh."

"Oh." Ellen sank slowly into her chair. "Nothing really. He asked me to marry him. I said no."

"You turned him down?" Jan's squeal of shock reached dog-whistle pitch.

"That's what I said. You want to go after him? Be my guest."

Ellen picked up a notebook full of notes about concert security and leafed through it. She heard the door shut when Jan finally left, and still she couldn't decipher the meaning of anything she'd written. Even though her life was now officially back to normal, with no sheikhs wreaking havoc in it, she couldn't shake the feeling that something had just gone very wrong.

The rest of the day Rudi walked the streets of New York. Omar and Frank walked a few paces behind him, Omar carrying the clothing Rudi had discarded.

Rudi thought as he walked. He thought about the things Ellen had said to him. He thought about the quarrel with Ibrahim that morning, and about all the other quarrels on all the other mornings. He thought about what he wanted for his life.

He had not gone to Ellen intending to ask for marriage. He had wanted only dinner, time spent together, the pleasure of her company. But when she talked of moving on, of ending things, sudden desperation had overtaken him. He could not imagine life without Ellen in it. Sheer panic had brought on his proposal.

Did he love her? Rudi had no idea. He had never thought much about love. He did not know whether he knew what love was, not love between a man and a woman. But the things he had told Ellen were true, and he had not told her half of what he felt.

Without her, he felt hollow. As if he had lost a part of himself. He needed her beside him, the way flowers needed rain and sun and earth to hold their roots. If that was love, Rudi did not like it much.

But perhaps Ellen was right. This feeling might be mere infatuation. If he did not see her, it might go away. The hollow inside him might fill itself, and he would again be whole without her.

How could it fill itself when he hadn't known he was half-empty until he met Ellen? How could he be whole when he lived a life he hated, when he hated the man he was while living that life? He could not ask any woman to share such a life, with such a man.

Rudi walked, and he thought. Until the streetlights went on. Until Frank made a cell phone call, huffing and hobbling several paces behind Omar. Until the car pulled up at the curb and Rudi got in, his decision made.

Two days passed in Ellen's new Rudi-free life. The problem was that, although Rudi's physical presence was conspicuously missing, his mental presence refused to leave her alone. She missed him with a bone-deep ache that worried her.

On the third day Jan buzzed on the intercom and announced that "a Mr. Eben Socker is here to see you," giving Rudi's family name her own unique pronunciation.

Ellen couldn't repress the thrill that ran through her. Rudi had come back. But the thrill turned to depression when she went to her door and saw Ibrahim ibn Saqr striding down the corridor.

"How can I help you, sir?" she asked, offering him the good chair.

She stayed behind her desk, feeling the need for all the authority, bogus or not, she could get. No wonder Rudi occasionally felt the need to slip free now and again, with this guy pulling the strings. Big brother intimidated her, and she didn't intimidate easily.

"Please, call me Ibrahim." He flashed a smile that was a pale imitation of Rudi's megawatt grin. "Our family name is often difficult for those who do not speak Arabic.''

''All right.'' She laced her fingers together in the precise center of her desk. ''Ibrahim. How can I help you?''

''I wanted to pay this visit to point out a number of things to you.''

''I see.'' The man made her want to grind her teeth, and he hadn't even reached his point yet.

''My brother Rashid appears to harbor some affection toward you. I thought it best if I made it clear that nothing could come of such an attachment. Our culture makes it difficult for a Western woman to adapt, and—''

''Hold it right there, Ibrahim.'' Ellen knew steam had to be coming from her ears. Ibrahim looked a little steamed himself by her interruption, but he would be grateful when she explained. She had to control her tendency toward smart-mouthing with this one, however.

''I'm sorry,'' she said. ''I don't mean to be rude, but your, um, clarification is coming a little late.''

''Oh?'' He steepled his fingers. Rudi had learned ''arrogant'' from one of the best.

''Your brother proposed to me two days ago.''

''I see.''

Ellen knew she shouldn't enjoy watching the man deflate as much as she did. ''Don't worry, sir. I turned him down.'' She told him the good news quickly, to make up for that guilty enjoyment.

''You did?'' Ibrahim looked astonished and relieved at the same time. Then he studied her with renewed appraisal. "Perhaps you are wiser than I thought."

Ellen rose to escort him out, before she strangled him with his power tie. "Did you ever think that maybe Rudi—Rashid is old enough to know his own mind by now? If you keep trying to push him into being somebody he's not, you might wind up pushing him away altogether."

Ibrahim glared at her, a thing he must have perfected sometime in his past. "Rashid is my brother, and by your own words, no concern of yours. Your opinions are not wanted."

"Sure." She offered her hand. "Good luck."

He scowled another moment, as if unsure whether her words meant something more than they appeared to. Then he shook her hand and departed.

The next Monday, Campanello came into Ellen's office. "Sheffield, we need you."

Ellen immediately went on her guard. Her boss never came to her, never said those words in that tone of voice unless he wanted something from her he didn't think he would get. "For what?"

"Prince Rashid's on the lam again."

"And what business is that of mine?" She took pride in the fact that her voice sounded cool even as her heart did panicky acrobatics.

"Okay, I know you resigned from the Qarif job." Campanello started up with that pitiful tone, the one that would make her agree to almost anything just to get him to stop it. "But I really need you, Sheffield. I got the big guy sitting in my office about to blow a gasket. He's convinced you plotted something with baby brother. Maybe he thinks you've got him tucked up your sleeve or something, but he's giving me all kinds of grief.''

"This is my problem because...?" Her heart was still bouncing off all her other internal organs, churning things up in there until her entire abdominal cavity felt tied in knots.

"Come on, Ellen. *Please.*" He shut her office door. "You want me to beg? Is that what you want? I'm already begging. You want I should get down on my knees?" Vic Campanello started down slowly to his creaky, forty-year-old, ex-cop knees. He truly was desperate.

"Damn it, Vic, don't do this to me. Get up." Ellen stomped around her desk and hauled him back upright. "You manipulative weasel. If I didn't like you so much, I'd hate you."

"I'm sorry, Ellen." He held on to her hand, watching her closely with those knowing cop's eyes. He'd learned to read her too well, back when they'd been partners, before he bought the business and hired her away from the police department with a big title and puny salary. "I know this hurts you, and you know I wouldn't ask if I didn't have to. I'll keep your involvement as limited as possible. You pinpoint, we'll reel him in. I won't ask you to be the bait."

"It wouldn't work anyway." She shook her head as she lifted her gray suit jacket off the coatrack and slipped it on. "I have a bad feeling about this one, partner. He's not going to be easy to find."

"Then I hope your intuition is wrong. Because two

more of those terrorists were spotted in town over the weekend.''

Fear drew its icy finger down her spine, stopping her heart in midflip. Rudi had picked a terrible time to skip.

Nine

It took a good half hour to calm Ibrahim down and convince him that Ellen had had nothing to do with Rudi's disappearance. Finally they got the story out of him. During a Sunday-afternoon visit to Bloomingdale's in full Arabic dress, Rudi's bodyguards had gotten a few paces away in the crowd of shoppers. When they'd caught up with him, they'd discovered another man behind the kaffiyeh.

After some confused dashing around, Frank had realized that Rudi had borrowed a trick from a movie and paid three or four men to come into the store, dressed in kaffiyeh and djellaba, and act as decoys. By the time the bodyguards had caught on, Rudi had vanished.

Over the next forty-eight hours Ellen and Campanello learned that Rudi had gathered several thousand dollars in cash during the past week, and that he had not left New York by air, train, or bus. Nor had he rented a car.

Time wore on. They visited one hotel after another—fancy expensive ones, middle-class ordinary ones, even fleabags. No one recognized Rudi from his picture.

By the time the second week rolled around, Ellen was firmly convinced Rudi was no longer in New York. She didn't think he'd left the country, but she had no logical reason for either belief. She called Buckingham again and again, talking to Rudi's sister-in-law, to Annabelle, the mayor, the bodyguards, to anyone Rudi might have contacted. But none of them knew anything.

The terrorists had vanished as completely as Rudi, as if they had shown themselves merely in order to inform their prey of their presence. Now Ibrahim and his bodyguards wasted half their time looking over their shoulders, and the other half worrying about the family hidden in Buckingham.

Late in the fourth week of the search, Ellen stared at her computer screen, her eyes burning, unable to read anything displayed there. She blinked, and the words became momentarily clear, then blurred again. It wasn't late, only about eight o'clock. Her eyes shouldn't be so tired.

She swiped the back of her hand across one eye, and it came away wet. Her cheeks were wet, too. Both of them.

Because you're crying, you idiot. Don't be so sur-

prised. The fear and worry she'd been denying surged up like a tidal wave and dragged her under. Unable to fight it any longer, Ellen folded her arms on her desk, laid her head on them and cried like a terrified child.

What if her search led the terrorists to Rudi? What if they had no clue at all where he might be, but her poking and probing told them where to look? Maybe she should stop the searching, just let him go. He had a right to live the life he chose.

But what if she stopped looking and they found him anyway? What if they found him before she did? Rudi was alone. He would make a perfect target for these terrorists, these cowards who had threatened the family members of Qarif's ruler, hoping to force him to accede to their demands.

An image flashed into her mind of a body falling. She thrust it away. Another image followed, one she couldn't banish as easily, one that had haunted her for more than a month. In it, Rudi laughed, head back and teeth flashing, his whole body caught up in his laughter, full of life and his joy in living it.

This time, when the pain and longing swept over her, Ellen gave up. She couldn't fight it anymore. She was in love with Rudi. Hopelessly, desperately lost in love.

She'd thrown away her chance at happiness. He was lost to her. But the thought of the world without Rudi in it somewhere hurt so badly, it had shown her how deep she'd fallen. She had to find him because he had to live. The terrorists could not find him first.

It was not an option. Rudi needed protection, no matter how much he resented the presence of bodyguards.

He had been gone almost a month. Even living frugally, he would be running out of the money he'd taken with him. Ibrahim had told them that on all his previous disappearances, Rudi had returned to the fold when his money ran out. Ibrahim remained confident Rudi would do so again this time. The huge amount of cash Rudi had taken with him had been Ibrahim's primary concern because it would allow for a longer absence. Ellen, however, believed that this exit was different. She was convinced that Rudi had no intention of coming back, not any time soon.

She dialed into a new database and put in her request. Rudi would have to find employment if he wanted to live on his own. He might even try to find work in one of the fields for which he'd been trained. She left her search running and headed home for another night of sleepless ceiling-staring.

The weekend played havoc with Ellen's search and her peace of mind. No one was in at any of the offices or search companies she called. Rudi remained missing. Finally, Monday morning, she got her hands on the documents she wanted, the names of all the pipeline and drilling companies nationwide.

There were hundreds of them, but not the thousands she'd feared. Ellen picked up the phone and began to call, beginning with those closest to New York, asking if they'd hired any new engineers in the past month, making up lies to explain her questions. If a human resources department proved reluc-

tant, she'd change her voice and make up new lies
when she called back.

Another week was half over when a helpful assistant to the assistant personnel director for a pipeline
company in Tulsa, Oklahoma, told Ellen that a Mr.
Rudolph al Mukhtar had started work there only two
weeks before. Al Mukhtar was in the list of Rudi's
names. Ellen wasn't positive, but it was the best clue
she had to Rudi's whereabouts. The only clue.

She thanked the assistant politely as she noted the
name and address of the company on a sticky pad,
then hung up the phone. Ellen snatched up her purse
and headed out the door, barely remembering to remove her headset before it ripped itself off her head.

"Tell Campanello I have a lead," she said to Jan
as she hurried past. "I'll call him when I know something."

At her apartment, Ellen packed a small bag, making
sure all her permits were in order to check her weapons onto the plane, both the big SIG-Sauer automatic
and the smaller Colt revolver. Her phone rang while
she was packing, but she let her boss curse at her
answering machine. She was going to Tulsa no matter
what he said. Letting him rant directly would only
make his blood pressure worse.

She had to wait an hour at Kennedy for a flight to
Dallas-Fort Worth, which would connect her with a
puddle jumper to Tulsa, arriving at 10:00 p.m.

By the time she arrived, she was exhausted. Ellen
checked in to a motel not far from Rudi's possible
new employer.

Patience at an end, she called directory assistance,

but Mr. al Mukhtar's new phone number was unlisted. Even if she had the number, she couldn't call. What would she say?

Rudi, I was a fool.

To which he would say, "And your point is?" He would say, "Too late. You had your chance." Or maybe he'd say, "No, you were right. I only wanted your body. Don't bother me anymore." Or he might damn her for betraying him again and vanish. Again.

She wanted to find him right now, see with her own eyes that he was all right, know that this Rudolph in Tulsa, Oklahoma, was her own Rudi and not someone else's. But she had nowhere to begin except his work, where he wouldn't be until morning.

Ellen forced herself to shower and pick at a bacon, lettuce and tomato sandwich from room service. Then she lay down in the big empty motel-room bed and stared at the crack of neon-pink light seeping through the curtains.

By six o'clock she thought she might have slept two hours with all her tossing and turning. Further pursuit of sleep seemed futile, so she got out of bed, dressed and was in her rental car in the lot across the street from Rudi's possible place of business by seven o'clock. As the hour got closer to eight, the building parking lot filled up with people coming in to work: tall, lean men with weathered cowboy faces, young pretty women in brightly colored suits, balding men in wire-frame glasses and pen-filled pockets.

Then an electric shock ran through Ellen as she recognized the walk, the short, dark curls of the man striding into the building. It was Rudi. She'd know that back, that backside anywhere, whether draped in charcoal worsted wool as it was now, or in nothing at all.

Heat rushed her at that errant thought. She was here to protect Rudi, not jump his bones, she reminded herself. The reminder made her pick up her phone.

"Campanello," he said when Jan rang her through.

"I found him," Ellen said.

"Where?"

"Tulsa, Oklahoma. Gainfully employed with the Atcheson Pipeline Company."

"Don't tell me you're in Oklahoma."

"Okay, I won't tell you."

"Shut up, Sheffield. Does he know you've made him?"

"No." Ellen slid the seat back in her car, wanting to close her eyes for five minutes. But she didn't dare.

"Okay, I'll have a team there by tonight."

"Vic…"

"Yeah?"

Ellen sighed, not sure what she'd wanted to say. "Never mind."

"Don't give me that. You called me Vic. You always got somethin' to say when you call me Vic instead of boss, so you might as well just spit it out."

"I'm worried what will happen if we just swoop in and scoop him up. This isn't like all those other times his brother told us about. Most of those times he was probably at his place in New Mexico, but he can't go there to get away anymore, can he? He never used a different name before, never got an actual job."

"What are you saying, Sheffield? You think he's going to bolt if he spots you?"

She took a deep breath. "I don't know. Maybe. If he doesn't run the minute he sees us, then sometime after he's pulled back in, he'll vanish again. And the next time he runs, he'll be more careful, he'll plan better. Next time, we might not find him."

"Next time, it might not be our job to find him."

"True."

"Big brother's paying our bill."

"Also true. But can't we just watch him here in Tulsa? You could talk Ibrahim into leaving him alone. Rudi's not hurting anything. He's just working for this pipeline company."

"Sheffield, you met the guy. Do you really think anybody can talk big brother into anything?"

"You're right. Stupid idea." She slumped lower in her seat.

"Okay, okay. I'll try. I owe you. No guarantees. And I'm sending Frank and Tom out on the next flight. You can't watch him twenty-four seven." Campanello paused. "Ellen, I'll wait till tomorrow to tell big brother you found him, if you want, if you got something to straighten out with the guy."

"Thanks, Vic. I appreciate the thought, but don't bother." She wiped away a stray tear. "There's nothing to straighten out."

"You sure?"

"Yeah."

About mid morning Ellen got a coffee from the bakery in the strip mall where she was parked and sat on the hood of the rental to drink it. At lunchtime she saw Rudi appear among a small knot of people, laughing and talking to a pretty red-haired woman in the group as they all walked to a car and got in together. Ellen ground her teeth against the wave of jealous pain besetting her and managed to get her car started in time to follow them to a Mexican restaurant several blocks away. They all went inside, the woman virtually attached to Rudi's side.

What did you expect? You threw him back.

Ellen told her conscience to shut up as she parked in the store lot adjoining the restaurant. No suspicious vehicles followed, either to the restaurant or back again, but still Ellen waited until Rudi had returned inside the office building before driving up to the take-out window of the Burger Doodle on the corner. She hoped Frank and Tom would arrive soon. Her sleepless nights were beginning to catch up with her.

Ellen woke with a start to someone rapping on her car window.

A plump woman with a face younger than her steel-gray hair peered in at her. "Are you okay?" she shouted through the window. "Can I get you some help?"

A frantic look at the clock told Ellen it was a few minutes after five. Panic set in. She got out of the car and scanned the building entrance across the way.

"I'm fine." She spared a quick smile for the wonderful woman who'd awakened her. "I just fell asleep. Stayed up too late last night."

"If you're sure…" The woman turned away.

"I was just waiting for someone." Ellen walked to the curb, trying to see the whole parking lot. Decorative shrubbery blocked much of her view.

People streamed out of the building, heading to their vehicles, lining up at the drive waiting to exit onto the busy street. Ellen spotted the redhead climbing into a pickup, alone. *Good.*

She started across the street, running through a short gap in traffic to the center turning lane. Waiting for a break in the westbound traffic, Ellen saw Rudi leave the building. He walked down the steps and along the sidewalk to the side of the building as cars and pickups whizzed by between them. Twice she started to cross, only to be thwarted. Rudi got farther and farther away.

Finally the light changed at the corner, and she darted across, swerving between cars pulling onto the street. She saw a blue panel van sitting alongside the low hedge separating the parking lot from the sidewalk and glanced in the front window as she pushed her way between the bushes.

Two men, clean shaven, black hair, dark complexions, wearing blue work shirts. She cataloged them automatically in her mental files, still her practice after three years away from the police force. Her primary focus remained on Rudi.

He walked across the drive, heading toward an isolated car, keys in his hand. Ellen broke into a trot.

"Rudi!" She called to him. *What was she doing?* She'd just talked Campanello into trying to talk Ibrahim into leaving Rudi alone. She'd intended to watch from a distance, not chase him down in a parking lot. She had lost her mind yet again.

He turned. The smile faded from his face when he saw her, and Ellen's jog slowed to a walk, then came to a halt. She'd killed his smile.

"Ellen?" Rudi took a step toward her, uncertainty in his expression. But the longer he looked at her, the more his face closed down. "I will not go back."

"I had to tell them where you were, Rudi. I had to." She forced her feet to move again, to walk toward him. "Your brother was on the verge of a heart attack, he was so worried about you."

"Ibrahim always looks like that." Rudi glanced away briefly, before capturing Ellen's gaze again. "It is no good. I cannot live a life that I hate. I hate the man I was becoming—useless, good-for-nothing. A waste of time, my own and everyone else's."

"No, Rudi. You're not like that." She stopped near the back of the car where he stood, its neighbors already gone home.

"I was becoming like that," he said. "If you put handcuffs on me and chain my legs together, you can carry me onto the plane and take me back. But I will not stay. It has become a prison to me."

"I'm not the one you need to be saying this to. I believe you. But you have to come back and tell your brother. Tell your father."

"What does it matter to you? You care only because you are paid to care. Without my father's money, you would watch me die in the street and not lift a finger."

"That's not true!"

"Isn't it?"

As he turned away, keys out to unlock the car, the image of the men in the blue van sprang to mind, and she felt the internal click as a pattern slid into place. The men matched the pictures she'd seen of the terrorists, though they'd shaved off their mustaches as a disguise. Their attention had been focused in this direction, as if anticipating...

"Don't touch the car!" Ellen leapt as she shouted, shoving Rudi onto the grassy median and rolling with him to the far side. Time seemed to slow. Her heart pounded five times, six. Then the bomb blast hit her, knocking her head into the concrete. Everything went gray and blurry.

The explosion startled Rudi. Then it made him angry.

He lifted his head, hoping to see a car or a license plate, and he saw two men getting out of a van, guns in their hands. Rising to a crouch, he glanced at Ellen. She struggled, her legs moving feebly, and she groped in the small of her back, but could not grasp her weapon. She was injured.

Rudi drew the big pistol in her stead and fired at the onrushing men. Wishing he had spent more time at the practice range during his last training session with the military, he fired again as he helped Ellen up and guided her behind a pickup truck in the next aisle.

"Ellen, where are you hurt?" He raked his gaze over her, looking for blood.

"What?" She frowned at him, then flinched as a short burst of gunfire ricocheted around them.

It cut off abruptly, and Rudi could hear the terrorists arguing. He peered over the truck, hearing sirens screaming in the near distance, and saw one of the men gesturing back toward the getaway vehicle, while the other kept swinging his machine gun in Rudi's direction. They had brought harm to Ellen.

Bracing the heavy gun, very similar to his own, on the hood of the truck, he took careful aim and fired at the more belligerent of the two. The man dropped like a rock.

The other turned to run. Rudi fired a warning shot and called for him to stop. "I did not kill your friend," he said in his own language. "But I will kill you. You know that I can."

The man halted. He dropped his weapon and raised his hands in the air, head hunched down as if expecting the fatal shot at any moment. Just then, what seemed to be twoscore police cars came screaming into the parking lot. Rudi laid Ellen's gun on the truck and lifted his hands as well.

"Rudi." Ellen tugged at his pants leg.

"Yes, Ellen?" He knelt beside her, cupping her cheek for support when she did not seem able to hold her head up on her own.

"Are you hurt?"

"No, *zahra*. I am well. Where are you hurt?"

She touched her head, and now Rudi could see the swelling, huge and red, above her temple. He started up to call for the ambulance, but Ellen caught his shirt collar and tugged him back.

"I was so worried," she whispered. The tears in her voice and pooled in her eyes shocked Rudi. He did not understand.

"Because you are paid to protect me," he said, trying to make things clear in his mind.

"Because I'd rather die than let anything happen to you." She tugged at his collar again. "Are you sure you're not hurt?"

"I am not hurt, my Ellen. But you are." He stood, lifting her in his arms. The authorities waited, allowed him to carry Ellen to the nearby ambulance, apparently informed of his role in the incident by the onlookers now crowding around.

Rudi identified Ellen. He identified himself only as Rudolph al Mukhtar. No one here knew any different, other than Ellen and the two criminals. There would be time enough later for the police to know his true name. He rode in the ambulance with her to the hospital, where he gave his statement to the police. He allowed the medical personnel to tend to his scrapes and cuts.

The two terrorists captured were only a small part of the gang of thugs ranged against his father. They would provide valuable information, particularly since they had set off their bomb in Oklahoma, a state with good reason to hate bombers. But it would take time to capture the entire group. And for all of that time, if he allowed Ellen to remain near him, she would be in terrible danger. She had already risked her life to save his. By her own words, she would do it again, as a matter of honor at the very least.

Ellen thought it was her job to protect him. But she was wrong.

When the doctors released her, mostly because she refused to stay "just in case," Ellen went looking for Rudi. All of the things she'd said to him, all of the things she hadn't let Ibrahim say were still true. Nothing had changed. But still, she had to see him, had to see with her own eyes that he was unharmed. She found him with Frank and Tom, his bodyguards, in the waiting room.

"We waited to see if you needed a lift to the hotel," Frank said, getting to his feet. "Besides, the prince wouldn't leave. We didn't figure it would be a good idea to knock him out and carry him off after these guys just tried to blow him up."

Ellen scarcely heard him, all her attention was so focused on Rudi. He looked worn, almost haggard, with circles under his eyes and an incipient beard shadowing his face. Then he saw her and smiled, and all her good, logical intentions vanished like fog in the sunshine, especially when she saw the worry tucked behind the smile. Could he truly care for her?

"Are you well, *zahra?*" His hand rose toward the bump on her head, paused when he glanced at the bodyguards, then retreated.

"Well enough that they turned me loose." Ellen tried to make her smile big enough to encompass all three men, but she failed. It was for Rudi alone.

"The police found your car and brought your bag." Rudi took it from a ferociously scowling Frank and handed it to her. "The rental company will pick up the car in the morning."

Ellen glanced at Frank. He was still scowling. Why?

Rudi took her arm, drawing her attention back. "Are you sure you feel well enough to return to the hotel?"

"I'm fine." The light-headed feeling had nothing to do with banging her head on concrete. It was all Rudi.

His arm beneath hers for support, he directed her steps to the door, to the large sedan waiting outside. Inside the car, Rudi urged her head over onto his shoulder. "Rest," he said.

She let her eyes close. Frank and Tom would watch, would give her time to think. But all she could think of was Rudi: her terror as he turned to open the car door, her relief at finding him safe, her contentment at this moment nestled close to him, with his hand resting on her knee.

His hand on her knee. The touch warmed all the cold, frightened places inside her. It loosened the knots of worry and set her free. So what if it hurt when he left her? She was hurting now, in her heart much more than her banged-up head. And maybe he wouldn't leave.

She'd sent him away before. Maybe if she asked for a second chance, showed him she believed in him, maybe he would stay. Even if only for a day, that was more than she had now.

Ellen curved her hand around his muscular arm and

snuggled closer. She could feel Rudi's smile against her forehead.

"Are you comfortable, *zahra*?"

"Mmm." She didn't want to waste energy in talking. Not just yet.

Sitting so close reminded her of that one wonderful night, when she'd been able to believe in fairy tales for a few short hours. A night when Rudi had made all her most secret dreams come true. And she wondered.

According to those who knew, lightning often struck the same place twice. More than twice, sometimes. Her free hand slid down onto Rudi's lap and she tucked her fingers between his legs. Rudi tensed a brief second, then he relaxed, and his hand on her knee slid a bit higher. She could feel the fires start to burn inside her again. Whatever else happened between them, she wanted a chance to see if what the experts said about lightning was true.

Ten

At the hotel, Rudi got out of the car to escort Ellen to her room, ignoring Frank's gruff instructions to stay put. Rudi would allow no one else to care for his tough, fragile city flower. And despite his resolve to remain strong and protect Ellen from her virtues, the drive from the hospital had proved him the weak man he was. He must have one last kiss from her pink, petal lips.

She clung to his arm through the small lobby, hugging it close as they walked up the stairs, Frank trailing behind. The pressure of her soft breast against his arm would drive him mad if he allowed it to. But he was stronger than his passions. One kiss. Then he would leave.

By the time Ellen stopped outside her room and handed Rudi the key, he was offering thanks for

Frank's glowering presence. The bodyguard would not allow Rudi to forget himself or Ellen's injuries. Perhaps it would be better to forgo the kiss.

Rudi slipped the card key through the lock and opened the door, but instead of walking through it alone, Ellen tugged on his arm.

"Ellen, I do not think—"

"Then don't." She grabbed his collar and backed into the room, dragging him after her.

"—this is a wise decision," Rudi finished as the door swung heavily shut behind him.

"I don't care."

In the dim entry light of the cookie-cutter room, Ellen looked up at him. Her expression softened, and for the first time he saw her without disguise or tension, the woman he had somehow known he would find behind her mask—strong, soft, tenderhearted. He could only gaze back into her summer-blue eyes.

Her hand rose, stroked gently across his cheek. "You scared me half to death," she said in a whisper-soft caress of her voice.

"You can see I am not hurt." Rudi caught her hand, intending to set her away from him. Instead he pressed her palm to his lips and held it there.

"I see. But I can't quite believe it." She ran her other hand down his chest, shaping her touch to his form. "I have a whole month of worry to make up for. I feel like I've been searching for you my whole life. I would think I saw you on the street, but it was never you. It's going to take more than just seeing to believe I've found you."

Shuddering with the effort to maintain control,

Rudi could not stop her hands as Ellen moved them from his mouth to the back of his head, from his chest around his waist to his back. He could only hold himself rigidly still as she stepped closer, pressed her sweet body against his. Then she lifted her face, like a flower to the sun, and kissed him.

The first touch of her lips shook him. The delicate thrust of her tongue shattered his control into a million glittering pieces. His arms whipped around her, crushing her to him as he plundered her mouth, tasting deep, needing more. When Ellen added her passion to his own, Rudi was far too weak to resist.

He lifted her in his arms, unable, unwilling to end the kiss. He carried her to the bed, where he laid her gently down. "How is your head?" he whispered. "I do not wish to hurt you."

"The only way you'll hurt me," Ellen said, twining her arms around his neck, "is if you stop. Don't leave me."

"No."

Rudi touched his mouth gently to hers, deepening the kiss as his fingers traveled from button to button, opening her shirt and laying bare her beauty. He couldn't stop kissing her to look. As she had said, seeing was not enough. He had seen her, could still summon her image to his mind, savor the delight of her beauty. He needed to touch her, to curve his hands over the soft, high roundness of her breasts, along the sweet sweep of her waist, over the delicate hollow between her hipbones. Then perhaps he could believe she was real and in his arms.

He stripped away her clothes, then assisted her in removing his own, never ceasing his kiss or the driving thrust of his tongue into her mouth. He tried to wait, to bring her passion equal to his own, but when he sent his fingers delicately seeking her hidden places, he found her slick and ready, waiting for him. Barely able to take time to protect her, Rudi slid home.

At that moment, he knew. Ellen was his home, the only one he needed. She was his heart, the breath in his body, his beloved.

He whispered the words to her in his own language as he loved her with his body, too much the coward to bare his soul in words she could understand. She had already told him she did not, would not believe his words of love, but perhaps if he showed her...

Rudi whispered the truth in her ear, in words she did not know, while his body sang to her songs with a beat as old as life itself. His heart pounded double time as he laced his fingers with hers, holding her in place. He drove deep inside her, striving to touch her soul with each thrust. Her sighs and moans sang counterpoint to his slow, silent tempo. She danced for him, her hips rising to meet him, urgent and demanding. And finally, with a crescendoing cry, she raked her nails across his back.

Ellen throbbed around him, and Rudi lost all semblance of control, pounding into her like a madman. Her pulsing climax continued, driving him beyond madness into a passionate explosion of such power that his mind went white.

* * *

Outside the room, Frank knocked softly on the door, then looked at his watch again. He sighed and pulled out his cell phone.

"Park the car, Tom," he said when his call was answered. "He's still in there with her. After this long, you know he ain't comin' out. Rent the rooms on either side—pull out that diplomat thing if you have to—and get your butt up here."

He hung up the phone and sighed again. Then he leaned against the door, folded his arms across his chest and settled in.

Rudi lay beside Ellen, studying her face by the pink light filtering through the gap in the curtains. Dawn would break soon, and the neon's power would fade. He wondered if dawn's light would fade the power of the things they had known and felt in this room.

He thought not. His love for Ellen would not fade, but it had to change. He loved her. Therefore he could not put her life in danger. He could not allow her to put her body between his and those who would do him harm. Even if she were no longer employed as his bodyguard, Rudi knew it would make no difference to Ellen. If they were together and came under attack, she would act in the same manner.

Huge cracks opened in his heart as his eyes traced the straight line of her nose, the sweep of her eyelashes across her cheeks. He had awakened her twice more in the night, partly to follow the doctor's instructions and ensure that she would wake, but mostly to make love to her again. Each time proved sweeter than the one before. He stored up memories, knowing

that much time would pass before they could be to-
gether thus, before they could be together at all.
Chances were very good that he would never hold
Ellen in his arms again.

His mind told him it was better so. His heart
agreed, unwilling to put her at risk even as it
mourned. Rudi slipped from the bed, careful not to
disturb Ellen's slumber, and he dressed. He debated
leaving a note, but decided against it. She had never
spoken of love, save to deny it. Better that she continue on that path.

Quickly Rudi slipped from the room. Tom rose immediately from the chair beside the door where he
had been keeping watch. "Wake Frank," Rudi said.
"Tell him to take Ellen home when she wakes. You
and I are flying to New York."

Ellen woke to the sound of someone knocking on
the door. Out of rhythm with the pounding in her
head, it made her head hurt worse. She sat up, and
only then realized that she was alone and she
shouldn't be. At least, she'd hoped she wouldn't be.
But the room was empty. No friendly noises came
from the bathroom. Rudi had left her.

"Hey, Sheffield, are you alive in there?" Frank's
gravelly basso came through the door as he knocked
again. "Open up, or I'm gonna get the manager to
do it and make sure that bump on your head ain't put
you in a coma or somethin'."

Groaning, Ellen dragged on a T-shirt and yesterday's jeans and went to let Frank in. "Don't talk so
loud," she said, padding into the bathroom to splash

water on her face. "A concussion has a lot in common with a hangover."

"You sure you're okay, Sheffield? You wanta go back to the hospital and make sure?" Frank surveyed the room, taking in the crumpled sheets, ripped from their previously neat tucking, and turned a bland face back to her. Bless him.

"I'm fine. Where's—" She corrected herself before she could say Rudi. "Where's the prince?"

"He and Tom took the Learjet back to New York this morning."

"This morning?" Ellen looked up from rummaging in her suitcase. "What time is it now?"

"After one. You slept so long, I thought somethin' was wrong." Frank hesitated before continuing. "Prince Rashid said he was going back to Qarif this afternoon."

"I..." Ellen took a deep breath. "I see." She wrapped a clean pair of slacks around her underwear and stood up. "Did they catch the guys who blew up his car?"

"Yeah, I forgot. You were out of it when all that came down. Rashid used your gun to drop one of the guys. Didn't kill him, just shot him through the leg, neat as you please. Held the other guy till the cops got there right after. We weren't but a couple of minutes behind the cops. Followed the ambulance to the hospital."

"Mmm." Ellen turned toward the bathroom, then stopped, needing to know. "So did they say how they found him?"

Frank looked down, cleared his throat, and she

knew. He said it anyway. "They, uh, they followed you."

She nodded and escaped into the bathroom before Frank could see the tears filling her eyes and spilling over to run down her cheeks. She was the one who had brought bombs and destruction down on Rudi. And when the terrorists attacked, he'd been forced to defend himself and her, as well. She had failed, totally, completely, utterly. No wonder he was going back to Qarif. Who could want such a failure?

Ellen stood in the shower long after the last of the soap and shampoo vanished down the drain, trying to wash away the pain inside. It didn't work. The hurt lay too deep. Hot water couldn't touch it. Nothing could.

She journeyed back to New York, the ache numbing her to everything else. Somehow she would get through this. She'd survived heartache before, but before had been different. This time her own failure had cost her the man she loved. The fault was in herself, not in Rudi. He was everything she'd hoped and believed him to be—kind, generous, delightfully unpredictable. Knowing that she'd finally found her Prince Charming, her Prince Rudi, and had nearly cost him his life caused more pain than she thought she could bear.

Until the package with the cowboy boots was delivered to her office. She clutched them to her chest, as if they were stuffed toys, and cried until her eyes ached.

Rudi stared out at the ocean rolling into the sands beyond the palace walls. The moon rode high to his left, veiled by wisps of cloud, silvering the waves below. He thought of Ellen, and he missed her.

He had tried to join in the family conversation at meals, but his thoughts would wander off on their own paths. He attempted to take an interest in the business matters laid before him by Ibrahim or one of his other brothers, but these things had always bored him, and bored him more now. The only thing Rudi had found to capture his attention was the hunt for the terrorist faction that had sent its emissaries to blow up his car.

He sat in on interviews with the two men he had apprehended. He eagerly read every report and chafed to take part in the action. More than once, Rudi asked to be allowed to return to his military unit that was participating in the search, only to be denied. He felt useless, half a man. And so he sat on the balcony and brooded on his loss.

"Why do you sit alone in the dark, little brother?" Ibrahim's voice came from the doorway.

Rudi shrugged. Ibrahim had no interest in the truth.

"You did not eat at dinner tonight. Without food, you will begin to rattle like dry bones and frighten the women away." Ibrahim crossed the gap between them and leaned against the supporting pillar. Rudi could feel him watching and did not care.

"You worry your mother, Rashid," Ibrahim said. "And you disappoint our father."

"I have ordered my life to please them. What more can I do?" Rudi didn't bother to look at his brother.

"You can be happy."

Now he looked, his eyes a slitted glare. "No, I cannot. To make my mother and father happy, I have given up work that I love in order to do things I hate. I have given up my freedom to live like a caged bird, and I have given up the woman I love to live in solitude. How can you ask me to be happy? I am not a nightingale, brother. I am the falcon of our father's name. I will live in this cage you have built for me. But I refuse to like it."

Rudi turned and stalked away, through the house, past the gardens to the guarded beach, feeling Ibrahim watching him still. He needed the vastness of the ocean to ease the bars around him.

Autumn had fallen in New York, crisp and cool. The leaves in Central Park turned red, gold, orange, brown, just right for the video to be shot there today. Ellen gathered up her plans for security around the shoot, stuffed them in her soft-sided bag and pulled on her gray wool jacket with the fake lamb collar, ready to go supervise.

At that moment her intercom squawked "Incoming!" as the door to her office flew open. She jumped, whirling first toward her desk, then to the door.

Ibrahim ibn Saqr filled the doorway, his eyes blazing with anger. The beard was new, but the rest she remembered too well. Ellen glared right back at him. They were through. Everyone was back in Qarif, or was supposed to be. He had no right to be here.

"Sorry," she said, trying to keep the snap out of her voice. "I'm due on-site. You'll have to take your business to Mr. Campanello. If you'll excuse me?"

She walked toward the door expecting, or maybe just hoping, that Ibrahim would back out of the way. He didn't.

His expression softened, the scowl leaving his face, and when Ellen came within reach he caught her chin, tipping it up. She jerked away from his touch. He merely did it again, without comment. This time Ellen endured his scrutiny, too tired to keep fighting. She was too tired for much of anything lately.

"You look terrible," Ibrahim said, without releasing her.

"Thanks. Just what I wanted to hear." She tried to summon up her anger and found a spark. "Now, are you going to let go of me, or am I going to have to break your arm?"

The scowl came back as Ibrahim snatched his hand away. "You are beautiful, but you have the temperament of a viper. I do not understand why Rashid is so obsessed with you."

Loss pierced her, almost made her stagger. With an effort, she hid the pain by replacing it with anger. "Obviously you're wrong. He's not obsessed. He's in Qarif."

"And you are here. He does not eat. He does not sleep. He wanders the palace like a ghost, staring at the sea. He takes no interest in his work, or else—"

"More of that finance junk? Can't you people get it through your heads? Rudi hates that stuff. He wants to build things, to create something concrete and tangible."

Ibrahim glowered, probably because she had dared

to interrupt his high-and-mightiness. "His name is Rashid. Why do you call him this ridiculous Rudi?"

"Because he asked me to." Ellen accepted the stare-down challenge Ibrahim sent her. Moments later, Ibrahim was the one to look away.

"This month," he said, "our father asked him to supervise the drilling of a water well in one of the border villages. Rashid worked so hard, ten and twelve hours every day, that he nearly collapsed when the well was done."

She could feel Ibrahim watching her closely, and she hoped her worry didn't show. Why couldn't these people take care of Rudi?

"The family is concerned for Rashid's health," Ibrahim went on after a moment. "He is haggard, thin, with dark circles beneath his eyes." He paused a moment. "Rashid looks much the same as you."

Ellen shrugged, wishing she'd put on her dark glasses before leaving the building, before leaving the office. She knew how she looked, but couldn't bring herself to do much about it.

"This gives me hope that you hold the same feelings in your heart that Rashid holds for you," Ibrahim said.

She couldn't hold back the bitter laugh. "What feelings? Disgust? Contempt? I don't feel that for him at all."

"Nor does he feel so toward you."

"Oh, please. You don't have to lie. I led the terrorists to him. He had to defend himself when they attacked."

"Because you were injured while saving him from the bomb."

"Another piece of prime stupidity. I know how to fall. I failed, plain and simple. Why else would Rudi have left like he did, if he didn't trust me? If he didn't see clearly what I am?"

Ibrahim stared at her. "Perhaps he thought to protect you. The remainder of the terrorist faction is still at large."

"See? He thinks I can't even take care of myself." Ellen clutched her bag tighter and tried to push past Rudi's brother. "I'm going to be late. They'll be waiting for me."

"Someone else can see to your duties." Ibrahim plucked the soft-sided case from her hands and handed it to Vic Campanello, hovering anxiously in the hallway behind him. "I will pay for your time. I require your assistance now."

He stepped forward, forcing Ellen to back away or get a faceful of power tie, and shut her office door. "Do you care for my brother?"

Ellen shrugged, unwilling to share the secrets of her heart with anyone, much less this overbearing, pompous son of the desert.

Ibrahim sighed, running a hand over his neatly trimmed beard. "You and Rashid deserve each other, for you are both equally stubborn. I was almost eighteen years old when Rashid was born, and have been as much father to him as brother, taking over many of our father's duties because of the business of governing that burdens him. But I neglected to listen to our father's wisdom when he told me to let Rashid fly with his own wings. He is so very different from his mother's other sons...."

He shook his head, then looked up at Ellen. "I also failed to listen to your wisdom, and now I must repair the damage I have done."

"So what does all this have to do with me?"

"Rashid is unhappy. Because he is unhappy, his mother is unhappy, and when his mother is unhappy, our father is, also."

"I fail to see what could possibly have brought you all this way to see me. I'm sorry Rudi is unhappy, but there's nothing I can do about it."

"I believe you are wrong. I believe you are the only one who can help."

"I'm not," Ellen snapped. "I am the last person you should be talking to."

"I offer you the chance to prove what you say." Ibrahim reached into his inner jacket pocket, pulled out an airline ticket and offered it to her. "Come to Qarif. Talk to Rashid, to your Rudi. Ask him whether he sees you as a disgusting failure, or whether—as I heard with my own ears from his lips—whether you are the woman he loves."

Ellen stared at the ticket, but couldn't make herself take it. She couldn't make herself believe Rudi could have said what Ibrahim claimed he had. She didn't dare. Twice already she had lost him. Her heart would never survive a third time.

Ibrahim took the two steps necessary to reach her desk and slapped the ticket down on its surface. The emotional weight behind the slim paper folder made the noise seem to echo through her, and Ellen shuddered.

"Come to Qarif," Ibrahim said. "If you have the courage of your convictions. Come to Qarif, if you dare to take the chance that you might be wrong about Rashid."

She could feel Ibrahim watching her, but she could not take her eyes off that airline ticket. It wasn't the chance that she might be wrong about Rudi that frightened her, but the possibility that she might be right. She didn't dare....

"The date on the ticket is open," Ibrahim said, his voice matter-of-fact. "You may use it at any time. Or you may cash it in, if you do not care enough to come."

Ellen heard the door open and close and knew he was gone, but still she stared at the ticket. It wasn't that she didn't care. She cared too much. And she was afraid. Twice now she'd thought the words *I don't dare*. Ellen Sheffield, the woman who would try anything, who jumped out a window in her Wonder Woman boots, who climbed a cliff thirty feet high with only her hands and feet—this same woman was afraid of a little airplane trip.

Okay, so it wasn't just the flight. It was the man at the end of the flight. Cliffs and window jumping could only break her bones, hurt her physically. Rashid ibn Saqr ibn Faruq al Mukhtar Qarif had the power to rip open her very soul, because she loved him. She loved him enough to remember every single one of his names, for crying out loud. And he didn't love her back.

But what if he did? What if he was just as miserable there in his palace as she was in her tiny high-rise apartment? She found it hard to believe, but Ibrahim had given her the means to know for certain. If she had the courage to take him up on his challenge.

Ellen gritted her teeth. Did she dare? She could hear her brothers in her mind, clucking like chickens as they taunted her for her cowardice. She could see Rudi's mocking smile, the challenge in his eyes as he dared her to accept his ridiculous wager, as he told her, "You are afraid of what I make you feel."

He'd been right. And yet, when she had taken his challenge and dared to feel those things, they had been so much more than she could have believed possible. They had made the pain of his leaving so much worse. But to know so much joy, so much delight, wouldn't people pay any price? Didn't they, trying to find it in drugs or drink?

And if Ibrahim was right, if Rudi did care for her—she couldn't think the word *love* for fear she would jinx it somehow. She knocked on her wooden desk just in case. But if he did care, that meant she didn't have to endure the pain, that she could have the joy.

Hope hurt. Ellen had almost become accustomed to the ache of its absence, and now Ibrahim had made her hope again, stirring up the pain. He had dared her. She'd never backed down from a dare before, and she wouldn't start now.

Coward or not, she had to know the truth. With her knees knocking and teeth chattering all the way, she would go to Qarif and find it.

Eleven

Rudi sat with his face turned up to the sun, eyes closed, basking in the warmth, sheltered by the balcony wall from the chill north wind that had swept through only this morning. He should not have pushed himself so hard while drilling that well. He'd known it while he did it, but the work was the first thing he had found to take his mind off his loss. When he stopped working, Ellen intruded into his thoughts again, so he simply kept going.

The exhaustion that had overtaken him when the water flowed bubbling into the cistern had been a blessing as well, for when he dreamed of her, he dreamed they were happy together. Waking was the nightmare.

Now that he had some of his strength back, he could begin on the next part of the water project, piping it into the homes of the villagers. This time he would pace himself, at least as much as he was able.

He heard footsteps behind him, but didn't bother to open his eyes. He was convalescing. If he pretended to sleep, perhaps whoever it was would go away. The sun's warmth would soon send him to sleep for real.

"Rudi?"

His fantasies were improving. Ellen's voice sounded as if it were on the balcony with him. He brought her smiling face up before his mind's eye.

"Ibrahim told me you'd worked yourself to exhaustion, but I never imagined..."

The chaise where he reclined dipped as weight settled onto it, and his eyes flew open in shock.

This was no fantasy.

Rudi sat up, reached for her, needing to be sure. She caught his hand, gripped it tight. He touched her cheek, devouring her with his gaze.

"Are you real?" he whispered.

She must be. The rosy cheeks of his memory had vanished, replaced by pale hollows, with dark-circled eyes above.

"Ibrahim said I looked as bad as you do." She smiled, and his heart began beating again.

Strange that he had never noticed how it had failed to beat during all the time they were apart.

"But I think he's wrong," she went on. "You look much worse than I do."

"Because I missed you more."

"Did you?"

The uncertainty in her eyes tore at him, and he

reminded himself why he had left. He could not risk her life. He could not bind her with the truth, and yet how could he lie? Rudi answered her with a smile, unable to find words.

Yet his fingers spoke what his lips could not, tracing tenderly over the curves and planes of her face, sharper now with her thinness. He could not stop touching her.

"Why have you come, Ellen? To assist in the capture of the terrorists? We are very close, or so I am told."

"No," she said.

Still he caressed her, smoothing a finger across the sweep of her brow, down the line of her nose, along the ends of her eyelashes, making her smile at the faint tickle.

"Have you come to protect us while we lie asleep in our beds?" he asked.

Ellen shook her head. Then she leaned forward, taking his face between her hands as if to prevent his escape, and she kissed him, a sweet, passionless kiss. "I came on a dare," she murmured against his lips.

A dare. He should have known. Rudi thrust her away and stood, striding to the end of the balcony.

Ellen came after him. "Rudi—"

He spun around and put his hand over her mouth, harsh at first, but he could never be harsh with her. His touch gentled, became another caress sealing her lips. He didn't want to hear her reasons for coming. Whatever they were, they could not possibly be what he wished them to be.

"I missed you." The words came out, despite his intention otherwise.

Ellen opened her mouth to speak past his fingertips. Desperate to stop her, Rudi did the only thing he could think of. He kissed her.

One hand gripped her shoulder, fingers still alive with the feel of her mouth. He lifted the other to cup her head as the kiss softened, deepened. Ellen's mouth had been open, and he took advantage, his tongue joining in the kiss. Her tongue slid across his in welcome, and somehow, suddenly, his arms were wrapped tightly around her, crushing her softness against his body.

Rudi pressed his arousal hard into the soft cradle between her hips. He wanted her to know how much he had missed her, what her presence did to him. His long native tunic and the light trousers he wore beneath allowed more sensation, more of the feel of her body along his to reach him. He should send her away for her own safety, but he simply could not let her go.

It had been too many long days and even longer nights since he had held her in his arms. He loved her so, wanted her, needed her so. He could not think. He was caught up in the chains of his passion, and he realized, as her hands slipped beneath the bunched-up fabric of his tunic, so was Ellen.

The touch of her hands on his bare skin drove him to madness. Rudi turned her, leaning her back against the side wall of the balcony, and reached for her skirt. Today it was long and flowing, the soft folds lifting easily until he brushed her silken thigh.

He touched lace, then skin above the stocking, and he shuddered. He got both hands beneath her skirt as he kissed her, his tongue stroking in imitation of the act he was so desperate for. This was indeed madness. He retained only a semblance of control as he stroked up and around and down her thighs where they were bared above the stockings. Then Ellen untied the drawstring of his trousers, closed her hand around his aching flesh, and he lost even that semblance.

With both hands he tore the fragile-seeming garment that attempted to cover her sex. Stronger than it appeared, the elastic around one leg defied him, but it didn't matter as Ellen guided him inside her. With one thrust, he seated himself deep, the side of his face pressed against the rough plaster of the wall. His hands cupped her buttocks to hold her tighter. The glorious feel of her wet heat enfolding him told him of his careless neglect of protection, but he did not care. If he got her with child, he would have at least that link to bind her to him, no matter the miles between.

"Rudi," Ellen whispered, and touched her lips to the tender spot beneath his ear.

He captured her mouth in another kiss to prevent her from saying more. She twined her leg high around his back, hooking her toes between his thighs. Rudi groaned. His hips began to move, quickly finding the rhythm his body required. Ellen met him, thrust for thrust, until she sent her cry into his kiss and her climax demanded his equal response.

Long minutes later, when he finally began to catch his breath, Ellen's leg slipped slowly down the back of his until her foot reached the balcony floor. Only then did the realization of what he had done truly hit him, like a boulder to the head.

He had made love to Ellen on a balcony, open to the gardens in view of anyone who happened to look in this direction. He had made love to her standing up, fully clothed—or almost—and in such a hurry that he had not thought about protection until too late.

Rudi groaned, hiding his face in her neck. He could not bring himself to pull his clothing together, for that would require space between them, space that would allow him to see the anger in her face.

But the fingers trailing through his hair did not feel angry. They felt nice. Comforting. Contented. He took a deep breath, inhaling essence of Ellen.

"Rudi?" She spoke again.

He took another deep breath and let it sigh out. They would have to speak sometime. Now was as good as any.

"Yes, Ellen?" His words were muffled by her neck.

"You never did ask what the dare was that brought me here."

She twined one of his curls around her finger. He did not want to move, did not want her to stop, but it was time. He summoned up his resolve.

"No, I did not." Rudi stepped away from her, her skirt falling into place again as he did. He took a moment to retie his drawstring and smooth the tunic down over his pants, aware of her eyes watching him.

Ellen reached beneath her skirt and pulled off her torn undergarment, leaving it lying on the floor where she stepped out of it. His passion stirred as he watched her, desire lifting its head, but he could deny it now.

Her gaze caught his and held it. "I dare you," she said, "to ask me what dare brought me to Qarif."

Rudi shrugged. "What matters is that you are here. Is why of any importance?"

"Are you afraid to ask?"

She stepped toward him, and he backed away. Knowing what she did not wear beneath her skirt made it imperative that he keep his distance.

"Ask me," she said, taking another step.

"Ellen, if we are to talk..." He sent a significant glance downward. "Please, do not come closer."

"*Ask.*" She held her ground, her eyes insisting along with her voice. "I dare you."

"What brought you to Qarif?" He snapped the words out like the crack of a whip.

"Ibrahim dared me."

Rudi waited, refusing to ask for more.

Ellen sank onto the foot of the lounge and looked up at him. The vulnerability in her eyes made him want to kiss it away, but if he kissed her, it would not be enough.

"Ibrahim said I was wrong about why you left Oklahoma in such a hurry. He dared me to come here and prove that he was wrong and I was right."

"And are you? Right?" His heart began to beat harder with hope, though his head knew there was none.

"I don't know." She bit her lower lip to still its

quivering. "I can't— That was some hello you gave me, but I still can't quite believe…"

She stopped and took a deep breath. "Rudi, do you hate me?"

"What?" The word burst from him as her ridiculous question brought him to kneel beside her. Rudi took her hand and held it tight as he searched her face. "How can you believe such a thing?"

"I brought those terrorists down on you. They only found you because they followed *me*." Tears flowed down her cheeks faster than his fingers could wipe them away. "And then I was useless—worse than useless—when they came after you with their machine guns. I'm a failure, Rudi. How can you not hate me?"

"How can I hate you, when I love you, *zahra?*" He sat on the lounge and gathered her in, rocking her gently back and forth. "You saved my life when you pushed me away from the car explosion. You took my injury, my hurt upon yourself."

Rudi touched the spot on her forehead where she had hit it, knocking herself semiconscious, then he kissed it. "Will you not allow me the privilege of protecting my beloved, as a man should?"

Ellen sniffled, wiping her eyes on his shoulder. "You love me?"

"I do."

She punched him gently on the arm. "Then why did you leave? Why did you go away and leave me to wake up all by myself with Frank pounding on the door? I thought you were giving me another chance, and then you were gone before I could even take it."

"I am sorry, my flower." He kissed her forehead again. "I wanted to protect you. Only two of the terrorists were captured in Oklahoma. I feared if they came after me again, the next time they would not simply bump your head. I never meant to cause you any pain. I never dreamed that my leaving would do such a thing."

"You never—" Ellen sat up and stared at him in disbelief.

Rudi smiled, brushing back the hair that had fallen into her face. "You have never said that you care for me, my Ellen. I believe—now—that you do. But you have never said it."

"Oh, Rudi." Fresh tears welled up in her eyes. "I'm such an idiot. I—"

"Just say it. Please?" He needed to hear it. A man should be strong enough to say the truth without needing to hear the same words in return, but Rudi was not so strong.

"I love you, Rudi." She cupped his face between her hands. "I love you, Rashid ibn Saqr ibn Faruq al Mukhtar Qarif. I love you by whatever name you want to use. I love you wherever you are. I love—"

Rudi couldn't wait for more confessions of love. He kissed her, sharing with her all the feelings he'd kept imprisoned inside himself for so long.

"I want you to know, Rudi-Rashid," Ellen said when he finally let her go, "that no matter where you go or what you do, I can find you. I *will* find you. I've already done it more than once, so you know I can. You're never going to get away from me again. So you can just forget that 'I left to protect you' junk.

We'll just have to look out for each other. You got it?''

''In that case...'' Rudi placed careful kisses across her forehead, her eyelids, her cheeks, lining them up in rows. ''You should marry me. Since you have already promised that I have no escape. We should be equally bound, do you not agree?''

''Do you mean it?'' She looked up at him, eyes wide with uncertainty.

He sighed, exasperated. ''Ellen, I have already asked you once to marry me. This is twice. Do not make me ask you a third time. If I did not mean it, I would not ask it.''

''What about—?'' She waved her hand vaguely at the palace surrounding them.

''We have time to work out the details. Ibrahim dared you to come. My family will not object.'' He took hold of her shoulders and looked her in the eyes, letting his determination show. ''I insist that you make an honest man of me. Say yes, Ellen.''

She smiled, and his sudden worry left him.

''Yes, Ellen,'' she said.

Rudi lifted his eyes heavenward to offer a quick thanks before he wrapped her in a close embrace. Holding her tight, he pressed a kiss to the top of her head.

''I love you, *zahra*. And I swear that you will never have to go in search of this prince again. Where you are, there I will be, and wherever we are together, that will be home.''

* * * * *

THE FORTUNES OF TEXAS

invite you to meet

THE LOST HEIRS

**Silhouette Desire's scintillating
new miniseries, featuring the beloved**

FORTUNES OF TEXAS

and six of your favorite authors.

A Most Desirable M.D.–June 2001
by Anne Marie Winston (SD #1371)

The Pregnant Heiress–July 2001
by Eileen Wilks (SD #1378)

Baby of Fortune–August 2001
by Shirley Rogers (SD #1384)

Fortune's Secret Daughter–September 2001
by Barbara McCauley (SD #1390)

Her Boss's Baby–October 2001
by Cathleen Galitz (SD #1396)

Did You Say Twins?!–December 2001
by Maureen Child (SD #1408)

And be sure to watch for *Gifts of Fortune*,
Silhouette's exciting new single title,
on sale November 2001

*Don't miss these unforgettable romances…
available at your favorite retail outlet.*

Where love comes alive™

CALL THE ONES YOU LOVE OVER THE HOLIDAYS!

Save $25 off future book purchases when you buy any four Harlequin® or Silhouette® books in October, November and December 2001,

PLUS

receive a phone card good for 15 minutes of long-distance calls to anyone you want in North America!

WHAT AN INCREDIBLE DEAL!

Just fill out this form and attach 4 proofs of purchase (cash register receipts) from October, November and December 2001 books, and Harlequin Books will send you a coupon booklet worth a total savings of $25 off future purchases of Harlequin® and Silhouette® books, AND a 15-minute phone card to call the ones you love, anywhere in North America.

Please send this form, along with your cash register receipts as proofs of purchase, to:
In the USA: Harlequin Books, P.O. Box 9057, Buffalo, NY 14269-9057
In Canada: Harlequin Books, P.O. Box 622, Fort Erie, Ontario L2A 5X3
Cash register receipts must be dated no later than December 31, 2001.
Limit of 1 coupon booklet and phone card per household.
Please allow 4-6 weeks for delivery.

I accept your offer! Enclosed are 4 proofs of purchase. Please send me my coupon booklet and a 15-minute phone card:

Name: _____

Address: _____ City: _____

State/Prov.: _____ Zip/Postal Code: _____

Account Number (if available): _____

---

097 KJB DAGL
PHQ4013

July 2001
COWBOY FANTASY
#1375 by Ann Major

August 2001
HARD TO FORGET
#1381 by Annette Broadrick

September 2001
THE MILLIONAIRE COMES HOME
#1387 by Mary Lynn Baxter

October 2001
THE TAMING OF JACKSON CADE
#1393 by BJ James
Men of Belle Terre

November 2001
ROCKY AND THE SENATOR'S DAUGHTER
#1399 by Dixie Browning

December 2001
A COWBOY'S PROMISE
#1405 by Anne McAllister
Code of the West

MAN OF THE MONTH

For over ten years Silhouette Desire has been where love comes alive, with our passionate, provocative and powerful heroes. These ultimately, sexy irresistible men will tempt you to turn every page in the upcoming **MAN OF THE MONTH** love stories, written by your favorite authors.

Available at your favorite retail outlet.

Where love comes alive™

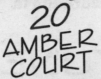